When I woke up the next morning, I knew two things right away.

One, I had not died of a heart attack in the night. And two, Sean Patrick O'Hanahan was in Paoli, while Olivia Marie D'Amato was in New Jersey.

That's three things, I guess. But the second two were totally random. Who the hell was Sean Patrick O'Hanahan, and how did I know he was in Paoli? Ditto the stuff about Olivia Marie D'Amato.

Crazy dreams. I'd been having some crazy dreams, that was all. I got up and took another shower, since the red mark was still there, and I couldn't wear the scoop neck. I decided to go for clean hair instead. Who knew? Maybe Rob Wilkins would offer me another ride, and when we were at a stop sign or something, he'd turn his head and smell me.

It could happen.

It wasn't until I was eating breakfast that I realized who Sean Patrick O'Hanahan and Olivia Marie D'Amato were. They were the kids on the back of the milk carton. You know, the missing ones. Only they weren't missing. Not anymore. Because I knew where they were.

WHEN LIGHTNING STRIKES

1-800-WHERE-R-YOU

MEG CABOT

WRITING AS JENNY CARROLL

Simon Pulse

New York | London | Toronto | Sydney

SIMON PULSE
An imprint of Simon & Schuster Children's Publishing Division
1230 Avenue of the Americas, New York, NY 10020
Copyright © 2002 by Meggin Cabot
All rights reserved, including the right of reproduction in whole
or in part in any form.
SIMON PULSE and colophon are registered trademarks of
Simon & Schuster, Inc.
The text of this book was set in Palatino.
Manufactured in the United States of America
This Simon Pulse edition January 2007
10 9 8 7 6 5 4 3 2 1
Library of Congress Control Number 2005937519
ISBN-13: 978-1-4169-2705-1
ISBN-10: 1-4169-2705-0

WHEN
LIGHTNING
STRIKES

CHAPTER

1

They want me to write it down. All of it. They're calling it my statement.

Right. My statement. About how it happened. From the beginning.

On TV, when people have to give a statement, there's usually someone sitting there who writes it down for them while they talk, and then all they have to do is just sign it after it's read back to them. Plus they get coffee and doughnuts and stuff. All I've got is a bunch of paper and this leaky pen. Not even so much as a diet Coke.

This is just further proof that everything you see on TV is a lie.

You want my statement? Okay, here's my statement:

It's all Ruth's fault.

Really. It is. It all started that afternoon in the

burger line in the cafeteria, when Jeff Day told
Ruth that she was so fat, they were going to have
to bury her in a piano case, just like Elvis.

Which is totally stupid, since—to the best of
my knowledge—Elvis was not buried in a piano
case. I don't care how fat he was when he died.
I'm sure Priscilla Presley could have afforded a
better casket for the King than a piano case.

And secondly, where does Jeff Day get off,
saying this kind of thing to somebody, especially
to my best friend?

So I did what any best friend would do under
the same circumstances. I hauled off and slugged
him.

It isn't like Jeff Day doesn't deserve to get
slugged, and on a daily basis. The guy is an asshole.

And it's not even like I really hurt him. Okay,
yeah, he staggered back and fell into the condiments. Big deal. There wasn't any blood. I didn't
even get him in the face. He saw my fist coming,
and at the last minute he ducked, so instead of
punching him in the nose, like I intended, I
ended up punching him in the neck.

I highly doubt it even left a bruise.

But don't you know, a second later this big,
meaty paw lands on my shoulder, and Coach
Albright swings me around to face him. It turned
out he was behind me and Ruth in the burger
line, buying a plate of curly fries. He'd seen the
whole thing . . .

Only not the part about Jeff telling Ruth she was going to have to be buried in a piano case. Oh, no. Just the part where I punched his star tackle in the neck.

"Let's go, little lady," Coach Albright said. And he steered me out of the cafeteria and upstairs, to the counselors' offices.

My guidance counselor, Mr. Goodhart, was at his desk, eating out of a brown paper bag. Before you get to feeling sorry for him, though, that brown paper bag had golden arches on it. You could smell the fries all the way down the hall. Mr. Goodhart, in the two years that I've been coming to his office, has never seemed to worry a bit about his saturated-fat intake. He says he is fortunate in that his metabolism is naturally very high.

He looked up and smiled when Coach Albright said, "Goodhart," in this scary voice.

"Why, Frank," he said. "And Jessica! What a pleasant surprise. Fry?"

He held out a little bucket of fries. Mr. Goodhart had mega-sized his meal.

"Thanks," I said, and took a few.

Coach Albright didn't take any. He went, "Girl here punched my star tackle in the neck just now."

Mr. Goodhart looked at me disapprovingly. "Jessica," he said. "Is that true?"

I said, "I meant to get him in the face, but he ducked."

Mr. Goodhart shook his head. "Jessica," he said, "we've talked about this."

"I know," I said with a sigh. I have, according to Mr. Goodhart, some anger-management issues. "But I couldn't help it. The guy's an asshole."

This apparently wasn't what either Coach Albright or Mr. Goodhart wanted to hear. Mr. Goodhart rolled his eyes, but Coach Albright actually looked as if he might drop dead of a coronary right there in the guidance office.

"Okay," Mr. Goodhart said, real fast, I guess in an effort to stop the coach's heart from infarction. "Okay, then. Come in and sit down, Jessica. Thank you, Frank. I'll take care of it."

But Coach Albright just kept standing there with his face getting redder and redder, even after I'd sat down—in my favorite chair, the orange vinyl one by the window. The coach's fingers, thick as sausages, were all balled up into fists, like a little kid who was about to have a tantrum, and you could see this one vein throbbing in the middle of his forehead.

"She hurt his neck," Coach Albright said.

Mr. Goodhart blinked at Coach Albright. He said, carefully, as if Coach Albright were a bomb that needed defusing, "I'm sure his neck must hurt very much. I'm quite certain that a five-foot-two young woman could do a lot of damage to a six-foot-three, two-hundred-pound tackle."

"Yeah," Coach Albright said. Coach Albright is immune to sarcasm. "He's gonna hafta ice it."

"I'm certain it was very traumatic for him," Mr. Goodhart said. "And please don't worry about Jessica. She will be adequately chastened."

Coach Albright apparently didn't know what either adequately or chastened meant, since he went, "I don't want her touchin' no more of my boys! Keep 'er away from them!"

Mr. Goodhart put down his Quarter Pounder, stood up, and walked to the door. He laid a hand on the coach's arm and said, "I'll take care of it, Frank." Then he gently pushed Coach Albright out into the reception area, and shut the door.

"Whew," he said when we were alone, and sat back down to tackle his burger again.

"So," Mr. Goodhart said, chewing. There was ketchup at the corner of his mouth. "What happened to our decision not to pick fights with people who are bigger than we are?"

I stared at the ketchup. "I didn't pick this one," I said. "Jeff did."

"What was it this time?" Mr. Goodhart passed me the fries again. "Your brother?"

"No," I said. I took two fries and put them in my mouth. "Ruth."

"Ruth?" Mr. Goodhart took another bite of his burger. The splotch of ketchup got bigger. "What about Ruth?"

"Jeff said Ruth was so fat, they were going to have to bury her in a piano case, like Elvis."

Mr. Goodhart swallowed. "That's ridiculous. Elvis wasn't buried in a piano case."

"I know." I shrugged. "You see why I had no choice but to hit him."

"Well, to be honest with you, Jess, no, I can't say that I do. The problem, you see, with you going around hitting these boys is that, one of these days, they're going to hit you back, and then you're going to be very sorry."

I said, "They try to hit me back all the time. But I'm too fast for them."

"Yeah," Mr. Goodhart said. There was still ketchup at the corner of his mouth. "But one day, you're going to trip, or something, and then you're going to get pounded on."

"I don't think so," I said. "You see, lately, I've taken up kickboxing."

"Kickboxing," Mr. Goodhart said.

"Yes," I said. "I have a video."

"A video," Mr. Goodhart said. His telephone rang. He said, "Excuse me a minute, Jessica," and answered it.

While Mr. Goodhart talked on the phone to his wife, who was apparently having a problem with their new baby, Russell, I looked out the window. There wasn't a whole lot to see out of Mr. Goodhart's window. Just the teachers' parking lot, mostly, and a lot of sky. The town I live in is pretty flat, so you can always see a lot of sky. Right then, the sky was kind of gray and overcast. Over behind the car wash across the street from the high school, you could see this layer of dark gray clouds. It was probably raining in the next county over. You couldn't tell by looking at those clouds, though, whether or not the rain would come toward us. I was thinking it probably would.

"If he doesn't want to eat," Mr. Goodhart said into the phone, "then don't try to force him. . . . No, I didn't mean to say that you were forcing him. What I meant was, maybe he just isn't hungry right now. . . . Yes, I know we need to get him on a schedule, but—"

The car wash was empty. No one wants to bother washing a car when it's just going to rain. But the McDonald's next door, where Mr. Goodhart had picked up his burger and fries, was packed. Only seniors are allowed to leave campus at lunchtime, and they all crowd the McDonald's, and the Pizza Hut across the street.

"Okay," Mr. Goodhart said, hanging up the phone. "Now, where were we, Jess?"

I said, "You were telling me that I need to learn to control my temper."

Mr. Goodhart nodded. "Yes," he said. "Yes, you really do, Jessica."

"Or one of these days, I'm going to get hurt."

"That is an excellent point."

"And that I should count to ten before I do anything the next time I get angry."

Mr. Goodhart nodded again, even more enthusiastically. "Yes, that's true, too."

"And furthermore, if I want to learn to succeed in life, I need to understand that violence doesn't solve anything."

Mr. Goodhart clapped his hands together. "Exactly! You're getting it, Jessica. You're finally getting it."

I stood up to go. I'd been coming to Mr. Goodhart's office for almost two years now, and I'd gotten a pretty solid grasp on how things worked from his end. An added plus was that, having spent so much time in the reception area outside Mr. Goodhart's office, reading brochures while I waited to see him, I had pretty much ruled out a career in the armed services.

"Well," I said. "I think I get it, Mr. Goodhart. Thanks a lot. I'll try to do better next time."

I had almost made it out the door before he stopped me. "Oh, and Jess," he said, in his friendly way.

I looked over my shoulder at him. "Uh-huh?"

"That'll be another week of detention," he said, chewing on a fry. "Tacked on to the seven weeks you already have."

I smiled at him. "Mr. Goodhart?" I said.

"Yes, Jessica?"

"You have ketchup on your lip."

Okay, so it wasn't the best comeback. But, hey, he hadn't said he'd call my parents. If he'd said that, you'd have heard some pretty colorful stuff. But he hadn't. And what's another week of detention compared to that?

And, what the hell, I have so many weeks of detention, I've completely given up the idea of ever having a life. It's too bad, in fact, that detention doesn't count as an extracurricular activity. Otherwise, I'd be looking real good to a lot of colleges right about now.

Not that detention is so bad, really. You just sit there for an hour. You can do your homework if you want, or you can read a magazine. You just aren't allowed to talk. The worst part, I guess, is that you miss your bus, but who wants to ride the bus home anyway, with the freshmen and other social rejects? Since Ruth got her driver's license, she goes mental for any excuse to drive, so I've got an automatic ride home every night. My parents haven't even figured it out yet. I told them I joined the marching band.

Good thing they have way more important things to worry about than making sure they get to one of the games, or they might have noticed a general absence of me in the flute section.

Anyway, when Ruth came to pick me up after detention that day—the day this whole thing started, the day I punched Jeff Day in the neck—she was all apologetic, since I'd basically gotten in trouble because of her.

"Oh, my God, Jess," she said when we met up at four outside the auditorium doors. There are so many people on detention at Ernest Pyle High School that they had to start putting us all in the auditorium. This is somewhat annoying to the drama club, which meets on the auditorium stage every day at three, but we are supposed to leave them alone, and they pretty much return the favor, except when they need some of the bigger guys from the last row to move part of a set or something.

The plus side of this is I now know the play *Our Town* by heart.

The minus side is, who the hell wants to know the play *Our Town* by heart?

"Oh, my God, Jess," Ruth was gushing. "You should have seen it. Jeff was up to his elbows in condiments. After you punched him, I mean. He got mayo all over his shirt. You were so great. You totally didn't have to, but it was so great that you did."

"Yeah," I said. I was pretty stoked to head home. The thing about detention is, yeah, you can get all your homework done during it, but it's still a bit of a drag. Like school in general, pretty much. "Whatever. Let's motor."

But when we got out to the parking lot, Ruth's little red Cabriolet that she had bought with her bat mitzvah money wasn't there. I didn't want to say anything at first, since Ruth loves that car, and I sure didn't want to be the person to break it to her that it was gone. But after we'd stood there for a few seconds, with her rattling on about how great I was, and me watching all my fellow detainees climbing into their pickups or onto their motorcycles (most of the people in detention are either Grits or JDs—I am the only Townie), I was like, "Uh, Ruth. Where's your car?"

Ruth went, "Oh, I drove it home after school, then got Skip to bring me back and drop me off."

Skip is Ruth's twin brother. He bought a Trans Am with his bar mitzvah money. As if, even with a Trans Am, Skip is ever going to have a hope of getting laid.

"I thought," Ruth went on, "that it would be fun to walk home."

I looked at the clouds that earlier in the afternoon had been over the car wash. They were now almost directly overhead. I said, "Ruth. We live like two miles away."

Ruth said, all chipper, "Uh-huh, I know. We can burn a lot of calories if we walk fast."

"Ruth," I said. "It's going to pour."

Ruth squinted up at the sky. "No, it's not," she said.

I looked at her like she was demented. "Ruth, yes, it is. Are you on crack?"

Ruth started to look upset. It doesn't actually take all that much to upset Ruth. She was still upset, I could tell, over Jeff's piano-case statement. That's why she wanted to walk home. She was hoping to lose weight. She wouldn't, I knew, eat lunch for a week now, all because of what that asshole had said.

"I'm not on crack," Ruth said. "I just think it's time the two of us started trying to get into shape. Summer is coming, and I'm not spending another four months making up excuses about why I can't go to somebody's pool party."

I just started laughing.

"Ruth," I said. "Nobody ever invites us to their pool parties."

"Speak for yourself," Ruth said. "And walking is a completely viable form of exercise. You can burn as many calories walking two miles as you would burn running them."

I looked at her. "Ruth," I said. "That's bullshit. Who told you that?"

She said, "It is a fact. Now, are you coming?"

"I can't believe," I said, "that you even care what an asshole like Jeff Day has to say about anything."

Ruth went, "I don't care what Jeff Day says. This has nothing to do with what he said. I just think it's time the two of us got into shape."

I stood and looked at her some more. You should have seen her. Ruth's been my best friend since kindergarten, which was when she and her family moved into the house next door to mine. And the funny thing is, except for the fact that she has breasts now—pretty big ones, too, way bigger than I'll ever have, unless I get implants, which will so never happen—she looks exactly the same as she did the first day I met her: light-brown curly hair, huge blue eyes behind glasses with gold wire frames, a fairly sizable potbelly, and an IQ of 167 (a fact she informed me of five minutes into our first game of hopscotch).

But you wouldn't have known she was in all advanced-placement classes if you'd seen what she had on that day. Okay, in the first place, she was wearing black leggings, this great big EPHS sweatshirt, and jogging shoes. Not so bad, right? Wait.

She'd coupled this ensemble with sweatbands—I am not kidding—around her head and on her wrists. She also had this big bottle of water hanging in a net sling from one shoulder. I mean, you could tell she thought she looked like an Olympic athlete, but what she actually looked like was a lunatic housewife who'd just gotten *Get Fit With Oprah* from the Book-of-the-Month Club, or something.

While I was standing there staring at Ruth, wondering how I was going to break it to her about the sweatbands, one of the guys from detention pulled up on this completely cherried-out Indian.

May I just take this opportunity to point out that the one thing I have always wanted is a motorcycle? This one purred, too. I hate those guys who take the muffler off their bikes so they can gun it real loud while they try to jump the speed bumps in the teachers' parking lot. This guy had tuned his so it ran quiet as a kitten. Painted all black, with shiny chrome everywhere else, this was one choice bike. I mean *mint*.

And the guy riding it wasn't too hard on the eyes, either.

"Mastriani," he said, putting one booted foot on the curb. "Need a ride?"

If Ernest Pyle himself, famous Hoosier reporter, had risen from the grave and come up and started asking me for journalistic pointers, I would not have been more surprised than I was by this guy asking me if I wanted a ride.

I like to think I hid it pretty well, though.

I said, way calmly, "No, thanks. We're walking."

He looked up at the sky. "It's gonna pour," he said, in a tone that suggested I was a moron not to realize this.

I cocked my head in Ruth's direction, so he'd get the message. "We're *walking*," I said, again.

He shrugged his shoulders under his leather jacket. "Your funeral," he said, and drove away.

I watched him go, trying not to notice how nicely his jeans hugged his perfectly contoured butt.

His butt wasn't the only thing that was perfectly contoured, either.

Oh, calm down. I'm talking about his face, okay? It was a good one, not habitually slack-jawed, like the faces of most of the boys who go to my school. This guy's face had some intelligence in it, at least. So what if his nose looked as if it had been broken a few times?

And okay, maybe his mouth was a little crooked, and his curly dark hair was badly in need of a trim. These deficiencies were more than made up for by a pair of eyes so light blue they were really pale gray, and a set of shoulders so broad, I doubt I would have been able to see much of the road past them in the event I ever did end up behind them on the back of that bike.

Ruth, however, did not seem to have noticed any of these highly commendable qualities. She was staring at me as if she'd caught me talking to a cannibal or something.

"Oh, my God, Jess," she said. "Who *was* that?"

I said, "His name is Rob Wilkins."

She went, "A *Grit*. Oh, my God, Jess, that guy is a *Grit*. I can't believe you were even talking to him."

Don't worry. I will explain.

There are two types of people who attend Ernest Pyle High School: the kids who come from the rural parts of the county, or the "Grits," and the people who live in town, or the "Townies." The Grits and Townies do not mix. Period. The Townies think they are better than the Grits because they have more money, since most of the kids who live in town have doctors or lawyers or teachers for parents. The Grits think they are better than the Townies because they know how to do stuff the Townies don't know how to do, like fix up old motorcycles and birth calves and stuff. The Grits' parents are all factory workers or farmers.

There are subsets within these groups, like the JDs—juvenile delinquents—and the Jocks—the

popular kids, the athletes, and the cheerleaders—
but mostly the school is divided up into Grits
and Townies.

Ruth and I are Townies. Rob Wilkins, needless
to say, is a Grit. And for an added bonus, I am
pretty sure he is also a JD.

But then, as Mr. Goodhart is so fond of telling
me, so am I—or at least I will be, one of these days,
if I don't start taking his anger-management
advice more seriously.

"How do you even know that guy?" Ruth
wanted to know. "He can't be in any of your
classes. He is definitely not college-bound.
Prison-bound, maybe," she said with a sneer.
"But he's got to be a senior, for Christ's sake."

I know. She sounds prissy, doesn't she?

She's not really. Just scared. Guys—real guys,
not idiots like her brother Skip—scare Ruth. Even
with her 167 IQ, guys are something she's never
been able to figure out. Ruth just can't fathom the
fact that boys are just like us.

Well, with a few notable exceptions.

I said, "I met him in detention. Can we move,
please, before the rain starts? I've got my flute,
you know."

Ruth wouldn't let go of it, though.

"Would you seriously have accepted a ride
from that guy? A total stranger like that? Like, if I
weren't here?"

I said, "I don't know."

I didn't, either. I hope you're not getting the

impression that this was the first time a guy had ever asked me if I wanted a lift or anything. I mean, I'll admit I have a tendency to be a bit free with my fists, but I'm no dog. I might be a bit on the puny side—only five two, as Mr. Goodhart is fond of reminding me—and I'm not big into makeup or clothes or anything, but believe me, I do all right for myself.

Okay, yeah, I'm no supermodel: I keep my hair short so I don't have to mess with it, and I'm fine with it being brown—you won't catch me experimenting with highlights, like some people I could mention. Brown hair goes with my brown eyes which go with my brown skin—well, at least, that's what color my skin usually ends up being by the end of the summer.

But the only reason I'm sitting at home Saturday nights is because it's either that, or hanging out with guys like Jeff Day, or Ruth's brother Skip. They're the only kind of guys my mother will let me go out with.

Yeah, you're catching on. Townies. That's right. I'm only allowed to date "college-bound boys." Read, Townies.

Where was I? Oh, yeah.

So, in answer to your question, no, Rob Wilkins was not the first guy who'd ever pulled up to me and asked if I wanted a ride somewhere.

But Rob Wilkins *was* the first guy to whom I might have said yes.

"Yeah," I said to Ruth. "Probably I would have. Taken him up on his offer, I mean. If you weren't here and all."

"I can't believe you." Ruth started walking, but let me tell you, those clouds were right behind us. Unless we went about a hundred miles an hour, there was no way we were going to beat the rain. And the fastest Ruth goes is maybe about one mile an hour, tops. Physically fit she is not.

"I can't believe you," she said, again. "You can't go around getting on the back of Grits' bikes. I mean, who knows where you'd end up? Dead in a cornfield, no doubt."

Almost every girl in Indiana who disappears gets found, eventually, half-naked and decomposing in a cornfield. But then, you guys already know that, don't you?

"You are so weird," Ruth said. "Only you would make friends with the guys in detention."

I kept looking over my shoulder at the clouds. They were huge, like mountains. Only, unlike mountains, they weren't stationary.

"Well," I said, "I can't exactly *help* knowing them, you know. We've been sitting together for an hour every day for the past three or four months."

"But they're *Grits*," Ruth said. "My God, Jess. Do you actually *talk* to them?"

I said, "I don't know. I mean, we're not allowed to talk. But Miss Clemmings has to take attendance every day, so you learn people's names. You sort of can't help it."

Ruth shook her head. "Oh, my God," she said. "My dad would kill me—*kill* me—if I came home on the back of some Grit's motorcycle."

I didn't say anything. The chances of anybody asking Ruth to hop onto the back of his bike were like zero.

"Still," Ruth said, after we'd walked for a little while in silence, "he *was* kind of cute. For a Grit, I mean. What'd he do?"

"What do you mean? To get detention?" I shrugged. "How should I know? We're not allowed to talk."

Let me just tell you a little bit about where we were walking. Ernest Pyle High School is located on the imaginatively named High School Road. As you might have guessed, there isn't a whole lot of stuff on High School Road except, well, the high school. There's just two lanes and a bunch of farmland. The McDonald's and the car wash and stuff were down on the Pike. We weren't walking on the Pike. No one ever walks on the Pike, since this one girl got hit walking there last year.

So we'd made it about as far down High School Road as the football field when the rain started. Big, hard drops of rain.

"Ruth," I said, pretty calmly, as the first drop hit me.

"It'll blow over," Ruth said.

Another drop hit me. Plus a big flash of lightning cracked the sky and seemed to hit the water tower, a mile or so away. Then it thundered. Really loud. As loud as the jets over at Crane Military Base, when they break the sound barrier.

"Ruth," I said, less calmly.

Ruth said, "Perhaps we should seek shelter."

"Damned straight," I said.

But the only shelter we saw were the metal bleachers that surround the football field. And everyone knows, during a thunderstorm, you're not supposed to hide under anything metal.

That's when the first hailstone hit me.

If you've ever been hit by a hailstone, you'll know why it was Ruth and I ran under those bleachers. And if you've never been hit by a hailstone, all I can say is, lucky you. These particular hailstones were about as big as golf balls. I am not exaggerating, either. They were huge. And those mothers—pardon my French—hurt.

Ruth and I stood under these bleachers, hailstones popping all around us, like we were trapped inside this really big popcorn popper. Only at least the popcorn wasn't hitting us on the head anymore.

With the thunder and the sound of the hail hitting the metal seats above our heads, then ricocheting off them and smacking against the ground, it was kind of hard to hear anything, but that didn't bother Ruth. She shouted, "I'm sorry."

All I said was "Ow," because a real big chunk

of hail bounced off the ground and hit me in the calf.

"I mean it," Ruth shouted. "I'm really, really sorry."

"Stop apologizing," I said. "It isn't your fault."

At least that's what I thought *then*. I have since changed my mind on that. As you will note by rereading the first few lines of this *statement* of mine.

A big bolt of lightning lit up the sky. It broke into four or five branches. One of the branches hit the top of a corn crib I could see over the trees. Thunder sounded so loudly, it shook the bleachers.

"It is," Ruth said. She sounded like she was starting to cry. "It *is* my fault."

"Ruth," I said. "For God's sake, are you crying?"

"Yes," she said, with a sniffle.

"Why? It's just a stupid thunderstorm. We've been stuck in thunderstorms before." I leaned against one of the poles that held up the bleachers. "Remember that time in the fifth grade we got stuck in that thunderstorm, on the way home from your cello lesson?"

Ruth wiped her nose with the cuff of her sweatshirt. "And we had to duck for cover in your church?"

"Only you wouldn't go in farther than the awning," I said.

Ruth laughed through her tears. "Because I

thought God would strike me dead for setting foot in a goyim house of worship."

I was glad she was laughing, anyway. Ruth can be a pain in the butt, but she's been my best friend since kindergarten, and you can't exactly dump your best friend since kindergarten just because sometimes she puts on sweatbands or starts crying when it rains. Ruth is way more interesting than most of the girls who go to my school, since she reads a book a day—literally—and loves playing the cello as much as I love playing my flute, but will still watch cheesy television, in spite of her great genius.

And, most times, she's funny as hell.

Now was not one of those times, however.

"Oh, God," Ruth moaned as the wind picked up and started whipping hailstones at us beneath the bleachers. "This is tornado weather, isn't it?"

Southern Indiana is smack in the middle of Tornado Alley. We're number three on the list of states with the most twisters per year. I had sat out more than a few of them in my basement; Ruth, not so many, since she'd only spent the last decade in the Midwest. And they always seemed to happen around this time of year, too.

And, though I didn't want to say anything to upset Ruth any more than she already was, this gave all the signs of being twister weather. The sky was a funny yellow color, the temperature warm, but the wind really cold. Plus that wacked-out hail . . .

Just as I was opening my mouth to tell Ruth it was probably just a little spring storm, and not to worry, she screamed, "Jess, don't—"

But I didn't hear what she said after that, because right then there was this big explosion that drowned out everything else.

CHAPTER

2

It wasn't an explosion, I figured out later. What it was was lightning, hitting the metal bleachers. Then the bolt traveled down the metal pole I was leaning against.

So I guess you could say that, technically, I got hit by lightning.

It didn't hurt, though. It felt really weird, but it didn't hurt.

When I could hear again, after it happened, all I could hear was Ruth screaming. I wasn't standing in the same place I'd been a second before, either. I was standing about five feet away.

Oh, and I felt all tingly. You know when you're trying to plug something in and you're not really looking at what you're doing and you accidentally stick your finger in there instead of the plug?

That's how I felt, only about times three hundred.

"Jess," Ruth was screaming. She ran up and shook my arm. "Oh, my God, Jess, are you all right?"

I looked at her. She was still the same old Ruth. She still had on the sweatband.

But that was the start of me not being the same old Jess. That was when it started.

And it pretty much went downhill from there.

"Yeah," I said. "I'm fine."

And I really felt okay. I wasn't lying or anything. Not then. I just felt sort of tingly and all. But it wasn't a bad feeling. Actually, after the initial surprise of it, it kind of felt good. I felt sort of energized, you know?

"Hey," I said, looking out past the bleachers. "Look. The hail stopped."

"Jess," Ruth said, shaking me some more. "You got hit by lightning. Don't you understand? You got hit by lightning!"

I looked at her. She looked kind of funny in that headband. I started to laugh. Once, when I went to my Aunt Teresa's bridal shower, nobody was paying attention to how many glasses of pinot grigio the waiter poured me, and I felt the same way. Like laughing. A lot.

"You better lie down," Ruth said. "You better put your head between your knees."

"Why?" I asked her. "So I can kiss my butt good-bye?"

This cracked me up. I started laughing. It seemed hysterically funny to me.

Ruth didn't think it was so funny, though.

"No," she said. "Because you're white as a ghost. You might pass out. I'll go try to flag down a car. We need to take you to the hospital."

"Aw, geez," I said. "I don't need to go to any hospital. The storm's over. Let's go."

And I just walked out from underneath those bleachers like nothing had happened.

And, really, at the time I didn't think anything had. Happened, I mean. I felt fine. Better than fine, actually. Better than I'd felt in months. Better than I'd felt since my brother Douglas had come home from college.

Ruth chased after me, looking all concerned.

"Jess," she said. "Really. You shouldn't be trying to—"

"Hey," I said. The sky had gotten much lighter, and underneath my feet the hailstones were crunching, as if someone up there had accidentally overturned some kind of celestial ice cube tray.

"Hey, Ruth," I said, pointing down at the hailstones. "Look. It's like snow. Snow, in April!"

Ruth wouldn't look at the hailstones, though. Even though she was up to the swooshes of her Nikes in them, she wouldn't look. All she would do was look at me.

"Jessica," she said, taking my hand. "Jessica, listen to me." She dropped her voice so that it was almost a whisper. I could hear her fine, since the wind had died down and all the thunder and stuff had stopped. "Jessica, I'm telling you, you're not all right. I saw . . . I saw *lightning* come out of you."

"Really?" I grinned at her. "Neat."

Ruth dropped my hand and turned away in disgust.

"Fine," she said, starting back toward the road. "Don't go to the hospital. Drop dead of a heart attack. See if I care."

I followed her, kicking hailstones out of the way with my platform Pumas.

"Hey," I said. "Too bad lightning wasn't shooting out of me in the cafeteria today, huh? Jeff Day would've really been sorry, huh?"

Ruth didn't think this was funny. She just kept walking, huffing a little because she was going so fast. But fast for Ruth is normal for me, so I didn't have any trouble keeping up.

"Hey," I said. "Wouldn't it have been cool if I'd been able to shoot lightning at assembly this afternoon? You know, when Mrs. Bushey got up there and dared us to keep off drugs? I bet that would've shortened that speech of hers."

I kept up in that vein the whole way home. Ruth tried to stay mad at me, but she couldn't. Not because I am so charming or funny or anything, but because the storm had left some really cool damage in its wake. We saw all these tree branches that had been knocked down, and

windshields that had been shattered by the hail,
and a few traffic lights that had stopped working
altogether. It was totally cool. A bunch of ambu-
lances and fire engines went by, and when we
finally got to the Kroger on the corner of High
School Road and First Street, where we turned
off for our houses, the KRO had been knocked out,
so the sign just said, GER.

"Hey, Ruth, look," I said. "Ger is open, but
Kro is closed."

Even Ruth had to laugh at that.

By the time we got to our houses—I mentioned we live next door to each other, right?—
Ruth had gotten over being scared for me. At
least, I thought she had. When I was about to run
up the walk to my front porch, she heaved this
real big sigh, and went, "Jessica, I really think
you should say something to your mom and dad.
About what happened, I mean."

Oh, yeah. Like I was going to tell them something as lame as the fact that I had been hit by
lightning. They had way more important things
to worry about.

I didn't say that, but Ruth must have read my
thoughts, since the next thing she said was, "No,
Jess. I mean it. You should tell them. I've read
about people who've been struck by lightning
the way you were. They felt perfectly fine, just
like you do, and then, *wham!* Heart attack."

I said, "Ruth."

"I really think you should tell them. I know

how much they have on their minds, with Douglas and all. But—"

"Hey," I said. "Douglas is fine."

"I know." Ruth closed her eyes. Then she opened them again and said, "I know Douglas is fine. All right, look. Just promise me that if you start to feel . . . well, funny, you'll tell somebody?"

This sounded fair to me. I swore solemnly not to die of a heart attack. Then we parted on my front lawn with a mutual "See ya."

It wasn't until I was almost all the way into the house that I realized that the dogwood tree just off the driveway—the one that had been in full, glorious bloom that morning—was completely bare again, as if it were the middle of winter. The hail had knocked off every single leaf and every single blossom.

They talk all the time in my English class about symbolism and stuff. Like how the withered old oak tree in *Jane Eyre* portends doom and all of that. So I guess you could say that if this *statement* of mine were a work of fiction, that dogwood tree would symbolize the fact that everything was not going to turn out hunky-dory for me.

Only of course, just like Jane, I had no idea what lay in store for me. I mean, at the time, I totally missed the symbolism of the leafless dogwood. I was just like, "Wow, too bad. That tree was pretty before it got ruined by hail."

And then I went inside.

CHAPTER

3

I live—since it's probably important to give my address in this *statement* of mine—with my parents and two brothers in a big house on Lumley Lane. Our house is the nicest one on the street.

I am not saying that to brag. It's just true. It used to be a farmhouse, but a really fancy one, with stained-glass windows and stuff. Some people from the Indiana Historic Society came once and put a plaque on it, since it's the oldest house in our town.

But just because we live in an old house does not mean we are poor. My father owns three restaurants downtown, only eight or nine blocks from our house. The restaurants are: Mastriani's, which is expensive; Joe's, which is not; and a take-out place called Joe Junior's, which is the cheapest of all. I can eat at any of them anytime I want, for free. So can my friends.

You would think, because of this, that I would have more friends. But, besides Ruth, I only really hang out with a couple of people, most of whom I know from Orchestra. Ruth is first chair in the cello section. I am third chair in the flute section. I socialize with a couple of the other flutists—second and fifth chair, mostly—and a few people from the horn section, and one or two of the other cellists who've gotten Ruth's seal of approval, but other than that, I keep pretty much to myself.

Well, except for all the guys in detention.

My bedroom is on the third floor. My bedroom, and my bathroom, are the only rooms on the third floor. The third floor used to be the attic. It has low ceilings, and dormer windows. I used to be able to fit my whole body in one of the dormer windows, and I liked to sit up there and watch what was going on on Lumley Lane, which usually wasn't very much. I was up higher than anybody else on the street, though, and I always thought that was kind of neat. I used to pretend I was a lighthouse keeper and the dormer was my lighthouse, and I'd look out for boats about to crash on our front lawn, which I pretended was a treacherous beach.

Hey, come on. I was a little kid back then, okay?

And, in the words of Mr. Goodhart, even then I had issues.

Anyway, to get to the third floor, you have to

take the staircase that is right inside the front door, in what my mom calls, in this French accent, the foyer (She pronounces it *foi-yay*. She also calls Target, where we buy all our towels and stuff, *Tar-jay*. You know, as a joke. That's how my mom is). The problem is, right off the foyer is the living room, which has French doors that lead to the dining room, which has French doors that lead to the kitchen. And so the minute you open the front door, my mom can see you, all the way from the back of the house, through all those French doors, way before you have a chance of making it up those stairs without anybody noticing.

Which was, of course, what happened when I walked in that night. She saw me and yelled—since the kitchen is actually pretty far away—"Jessica! Get in here!"

Which, of course, meant I was in trouble.

Wondering what I could have done now—and hoping Mr. Goodhart hadn't gone ahead and called her anyway—I put down my backpack and my flute and everything on this little bench by the stairs and started the long walk through the living room and dining room, thinking up a good story for why I was so late, in case that was why she was mad.

"We had band practice," I started saying. By the time I got to the dining room table—which has this buzzer built into the floor beneath the chair at the head of the table, so the hostess can step on it and signal to the servants in the kitchen that it's time to bring out dessert, which, since we have no servants, is just this huge annoyance, especially when we were growing up, since it's impossible for little kids to keep from buzzing something like that all the time, which drove my mom, who was usually in the kitchen, postal—I was rolling with it.

"Yeah, band practice went long, Mom. On account of the hail. We all had to run and stand under the bleachers, and there was all this lightning, and—"

"Look at this."

My mom held a letter up to my nose. My brother Mike was sitting, kind of slumped, at the kitchen counter. He looked unhappy, but then, he had never looked happy a day in his life, as far as I can remember, except when my parents got him a Mac for Christmas. Then he looked happy.

I looked at the letter my mom was holding. I couldn't read it, since it was too close to my nose. But that was okay. My mom was going, "Do you know what this is, Jessica? Do you know what this is? It's a letter from Harvard. And what do you think it says?"

I said, "Oh, hey, Mikey. Congratulations."

Mike said, "Thanks," but he didn't sound very excited.

"My little boy." My mom took the letter and started waving it around. "My little Mikey! Going to Harvard! Oh, my God, I can hardly believe it!" She did a weird little dance.

My mom isn't normally so weird. Most of the time she's pretty much like other moms. She helps my dad out sometimes with the restaurants, like with the billing and payroll, but mostly she stays home and does stuff like regrout the tile in the bathrooms. My mom, like most moms, is totally into her kids, so Mike getting into Harvard—even though it's really no big surprise, seeing as how he got a perfect score on his SATs—was this really big deal to her.

"I already called your father," she said. "We're going to Mastriani's for lobster."

"Cool," I said. "Can I invite Ruth?"

My mom made a little waving gesture. "Sure, why not? When have we ever gone out for a family dinner and not brought along Ruth?" She was being sarcastic, but she didn't mean it. My mom likes Ruth. I think. "Michael, perhaps there is someone you'd like to invite?"

The way she said "someone," you could tell my mom, of course, meant a girl. But Mike has only ever liked one girl his entire life, and that's Claire Lippman, who lives two houses over, and Claire Lippman, who is a year younger than Mike and a year older than me, barely even knows Mike is alive, since she is too busy starring in all of our high school's plays and musicals to pay any attention to the geeky senior down the street who spies on her every time she lies out on her carport roof in her bikini, which she does every single day without fail starting as soon as school lets out for the summer. She doesn't go back inside, either, until Labor Day, or unless a cute guy in a car drives up and asks her if she wants to go swimming at one of the quarries.

Claire is either a slave to ultraviolet rays or a total exhibitionist. I haven't figured out which yet.

Anyway, there was no chance my brother was going to ask "someone" to go with us for dinner, since Claire Lippman would be like, "Now, who are you?" if he ever even got up the nerve to talk to her.

"No," Mike said, all embarrassed. He was turning bright red, and it was only me and Mom standing there. Could you imagine if Claire Lippman had actually been present? "There's nobody I want to ask."

"Faint heart never won fair lady," my mom said. My mom, besides frequently talking in a fake French accent, also goes around quoting from Shakespearean plays and Gilbert and Sullivan operettas.

On second thought, maybe she's not so much like other people's moms after all.

"I got it, Mom," Mike said through gritted teeth. "Not tonight, okay?"

My mom shrugged. "Fine. Jessica, if you're going, allow me to assure you you're not going in *that.*" *That* was what I normally wear—T-shirt, jeans, and my Pumas. "Go put on the blue calico I made for Easter."

Okay. My mom has this thing about making us matching outfits. I am not even kidding. It was cute when I was six, but at sixteen, let me tell you, there is nothing cute about wearing a home-made dress that matches the one your mother has on. Especially since all the dresses my mom makes are of the Laura Ingalls variety.

You would think, considering the fact that I don't have any problem walking up to football tackles and punching them in the neck, that I wouldn't have any problem telling my mother to quit making me wear outfits that match hers. You would think that.

However, if your father promised you that if you wore them without complaining, he would buy you a Harley when you turned eighteen, you would wear them, too.

I said, "Okay," and started up the back stair-case, what used to be the servants' staircase, back at the turn of the century—the nineteenth into the twentieth, I mean—when our house was built. "I'll tell Douglas."

"Oh," I heard my mom say. "Jess?"

But I kept on going. I knew what she was going to say. She was going to say not to bother Douglas. That's what she always says.

Personally, I enjoy bothering Douglas. Also, I asked Mr. Goodhart about it, and he said it's probably good to bother Douglas. So I bother him a lot. What I do is, I go up to the door to his room, which has a big Keep Out sign on it, and I bang on it really hard. Then I yell, "Doug! It's me, Jess!"

Then I just walk in. Douglas isn't allowed to have a lock on his door anymore. Not since my dad and I had to knock it down last Christmas.

Douglas was lying on his bed reading a comic book. It had this Viking on the cover, with a girl with big boobs. All Douglas ever does, since he came home from college, is read comic books. And in all the comic books, the girls have big boobs.

"Guess what," I said, sitting down on Douglas's bed.

"Mikey got into Harvard," Douglas said. "I already heard. I expect the whole neighborhood heard.".

"Nope," I said. "That's not it."

He looked at me over the top of the comic book. "I know Mom thinks she's taking us all to Mastriani's to celebrate, but I'm not going. She's going to have to learn to live with disappointment. And you better keep your hands off me. I'm not going, no matter how hard you hit me. And this time, I might just hit you back."

"That's not it, either," I said. "And I wasn't planning on hitting you. Much."

"What, then?"

I shrugged. "I got hit by lightning."

Douglas turned back to his comic book. "Right. Shut the door on your way out."

"I'm serious," I said. "Ruth and I were waiting

out the storm, underneath the bleachers at
school—"

"Those bleachers," Douglas said, looking at
me again, "are made of metal."

"Right. And I was leaning on one of the sup-
ports, and lightning struck the bleachers, and
next thing I knew, I was standing like five feet
from where I'd been, and I was tingly all over,
and—"

"Bullshit," Douglas said. But he sat up. "That
is bullshit, Jess."

"I swear it's true. You can ask Ruth."

"You did not get hit by lightning," Douglas
said. "You would not be sitting here, talking to
me, if you'd been hit by lightning."

"Douglas, I'm telling you, I was."

"Where's the entrance wound, then?" Douglas
reached out and grabbed my right hand and
flipped it over. "The exit wound? The bolt would
have entered you one place, and left you in
another. And there would be a star-shaped scar
in both places."

As he'd been talking, he'd let go of my right
hand and grabbed my left, and flipped it over,
too. But there wasn't a star-shaped scar on either
of my palms.

"See." He flung my hand away in disgust.
Douglas knows about stuff like this because all
he ever does is read, and sometimes he reads
actual books, as opposed to comics. "You weren't
struck by lightning. Don't go around saying stuff

like that, Jess. You know, lightning kills hundreds of people a year. If you had been struck, you'd definitely be in a coma, at the very least."

He lay back down and picked his comic book up again. "Now, get out of here," he said, giving me a shove with his foot. "I'm busy."

I sighed and got up. "Okay," I said. "But you're going to be sorry. Mom says we're having lobster."

"We had lobster the night I got my acceptance letter to State," Douglas said to his comic book, "and look how that turned out."

I reached out and grabbed his big toe and squeezed it. "Okay, big baby. Just lie here like a big lump, with Captain Lars and his big-busted beauty, Helga."

Douglas looked at me from behind the comic book. "Her name," he said, "happens to be Oona."

Then he ducked back behind the comic book.

I left his room, closing the door behind me, and went up the stairs to my own room.

I'm not too worried about Douglas. I know I probably should be, but I'm not. I'm probably the only person in my family who isn't, except for maybe my dad. Douglas has always been weird. My whole life, it seems, I've been beating up people who called my older brother a retard, or a spaz, or a weirdo. I don't know why, but even though most of the time I'm way smaller than them, I feel obligated to punch them in the face for dissing my brother.

This freaks out my mom, but not my dad. My dad just taught me how to punch more effectively, by advising me to keep my thumb on the outside of my fist. When I was very little, I used to do it with my thumb on the inside. Consequently, I sprained it several times. My thumb, I mean.

Douglas used to get mad when I'd get into fights because of him, so after a while I learned to do it behind his back. And I guess it would be humiliating, having one's little sister constantly going around, beating up people on your behalf. But I don't think that contributed to what happened to Douglas later. You know, this past Christmas, when he tried to kill himself. I mean, you don't try to kill yourself because your little sister used to get into fights over you in junior high, or whatever.

Do you?

Anyway, once I was in my room, I called Ruth and invited her out to dinner with us. I knew that, even though today was the first day of what would be another one of her diets, thanks to Jeff Day, Ruth wasn't going to be able to resist. Not only was it lobster, but it was Michael. Ruth tries to pretend she doesn't like Michael, but between you and me, the girl has it bad for him. Don't ask me why. He's no prize, believe me.

And just like I knew she would, she said, "Well, I really shouldn't. Lobster is so fattening. Well, not the lobster, really, but all the butter . . .

but I guess it *is* a special occasion, what with Michael getting into Harvard and all. I guess I should go. Okay, I'll go."

"Come over," I said. "Give me ten minutes, though. I gotta change."

"Wait a minute." Ruth's voice grew suspicious. "Your mom's not making you wear one of those gay outfits, is she?" When I remained silent, Ruth said, "You know, I don't think a motorcycle is enough. Your dad should buy you a damned Maserati for what that woman puts you through."

Ruth thinks my mom is suffering from the oppression of a patriarchal society, consisting mainly of my dad. But that isn't true. My dad would totally love it if my mom got a job. It would keep her from obsessing about Douglas. Now that he's home again, though, she says she can't even think of working, since who would watch him and make sure he stays away from the razor blades the next time?

I told Ruth that, yes, I had to wear one of my mom's gay outfits, even though *gay* is the wrong word for it, because all the gay people I know are really cool and would sooner drop dead than wear something made out of gingham, except on Halloween. But whatever. I hung up and started undressing. I pretty much live in jeans and a T-shirt. In the winter, I'll put on a sweater, but seriously, I don't dress up for school like some girls. Sometimes I don't even shower in the morning. I mean, what is the point? There is no one there I want to impress.

Well, at least there *hadn't* been, until Rob Wilkins asked me if I wanted a ride home. Now *that* might be worth blow-drying for.

Only, of course, I couldn't let Ruth know. And she totally would, the minute she swung by to pick me up. She'd be like, "Mousse much?"

Although she'd probably approve—at least until she found out who I was moussing for.

Anyway, while I was undressing, it occurred to me that Douglas might have been wrong. There might have been a star-shaped scar somewhere else on my body, not necessarily on my palms. Say on the bottoms of my feet, or something.

But when I checked, my soles were just pink as usual. No scars. Not even any lint between my toes.

It was weird about Rob Wilkins asking me if I wanted a ride like that. I mean, I hardly knew the guy. We had detention together, and that was it. Well, that isn't strictly true. Last semester, he'd been in Health with me. You know, Coach Albright's class. You're supposed to take it as a sophomore, but for some reason—okay, probably because he'd flunked first time around—Rob had been taking it his senior year. He'd sat behind me. He was pretty quiet most of the time. Occasionally he'd have a conversation with the guy behind him, who was also a Grit. I'd eaves-drop, of course. These conversations generally revolved around bands—Grit bands, mostly heavy metal, or country—or cars.

Sometimes I couldn't help butting in. Like once I said that I really didn't think Steven Tyler was a musical genius. The artist formerly known as Prince was the only living musician I'd call a genius. And then, for about a week, we kind of dissected their lyrics, and Rob eventually agreed with me.

And once Rob was talking about motorcycles, and the guy behind him was going on and on about Kawasaki, and I was just like, "What are you, high? American, all the way," and Rob gave me a high five.

Coach Albright hadn't exactly been there in the classroom a lot. Football emergencies kept coming up, requiring him to leave us to work on the questions at the end of the chapter. You know the kind of questions. The spleen performs what function? The adult male generates how many sperm each day? The kind of questions you instantly forget the answers to as soon as you've passed the class.

I decided that, for school tomorrow, I might wear this Gap shirt Douglas had given me for Christmas. I'd never worn it to school before, because it had a scoop neck. Not exactly the kind of thing you want to wear while taking down a quarterback.

But, hey, if that's what it took to bag a ride on that Indian . . .

It wasn't until I was buttoning up my hideous lilac-colored Laura Ingalls dress that I glanced at my reflection in the mirror and saw it: this fist-sized red mark in the middle of my chest. It didn't hurt or anything. It was like I'd suddenly broken out in hives or something. Like someone had slipped a bad clam into my shells and sauce.

From the center of the red mark radiated these tendrils. In fact, looking at it in the mirror, I saw that the whole thing was . . .

Well, kind of shaped like a star.

CHAPTER

4

Ruth said, "I'm telling you, I don't see another one. There's just the one."

"Are you sure?"

I was standing, stark naked, in the middle of my bedroom. It was after dinner, which I guess had been delicious. I wouldn't know, having been unable to taste anything, what with my excitement over having been really and truly struck by lightning. The star-shaped burn proved it. It was the entrance wound Douglas had been talking about.

The only problem was, I couldn't find an exit wound. I'd made Ruth come over after dinner and help me look. Only she wasn't being much help.

"I had no idea," she said from my bed, where she was lying, flipping through a copy of *Critical*

Theory Since Plato—you know, just a little light reading—she'd brought over, "you'd actually grown breasts. I mean it. You aren't an A cup anymore. When did that happen?"

"Ruth," I said, "what about on my back? Do you see one on my back?"

"No. What are you now, a B?"

"How should I know? You know I never wear a bra. How about on my butt? Anything on my butt?"

"No. Is there something between a B and a C? Because I think that's what you are now. And you really should start wearing one, you know. You could start to sag, like those women in *National Geographic*."

"You," I said to her, "are no help."

"Well, what do you expect me to do, Jess?" Ruth turned grumpily back to her book. "I mean, it's a little weird, having your best friend ask you to check her body for entrance and exit wounds, don't you think? I mean, it's a bit *gay*."

I went, "I don't want you to feel me up, you moron. I just wanted you to tell me if you saw an exit wound." I pulled on a pair of sweats. "Get over yourself."

"I can't believe," Ruth said, ignoring me, "that Michael's going to Harvard. I mean, *Harvard*. He is so smart. How can someone so smart fall for Claire Lippman?"

I pulled a sweatshirt over my head. "Claire's not so bad," I said. I knew her pretty well, see, from detention. Not that she ever got detention, but they held detention in the auditorium, and Claire always had the lead in whatever play the drama club was putting on, so I'd watched most of her rehearsals when she played Emily in *Our Town*, Maria in *West Side Story*, and, of course, Juliet in *Romeo and Juliet*.

"She's a really good actress," I said.

"I highly doubt," Ruth said, "that Michael admires her for her *talent*."

Ruth always calls Mike Michael, even though everyone else calls him Mike. She says Mike is a Grit name.

"Well," I said, "you got to admit, she does look good in a bathing suit."

Ruth snorted. "That slut. I can't believe she does that. Every summer. I mean, it was one thing back before she hit puberty. But now . . . what's she trying to do? Cause a traffic accident?"

"I'm hungry," I said, because I was. "You want something?"

Ruth said, "I'm not surprised. You hardly touched your lobster."

"I was too excited to eat then," I said. "I mean, come on. I got electrocuted today."

"I wish," Ruth said, to the book, "you'd go to a doctor. You could be hemorrhaging internally, you know."

I said, "I'm going downstairs. You want anything?"

She yawned. "No. I gotta go. I'll just stop by Michael's room to say congratulations one more time, and good night."

I thought it would be best to leave the two of them alone, you know, in case there was a romantic interlude, so I went downstairs to forage for food. The chances of Mikey ever even looking twice in Ruth's direction are like nil, but hope springs eternal, even in the heart of a fat girl. Not that Ruth is that fat. She's just twice the size of Claire Lippman. Not that Claire is so skinny—she's pretty hippy, actually. But boys seem to like that, I've noticed. In magazines, they make out if you're not Kate Moss, your life is over, but in real life, boys—like my brothers—wouldn't look twice at Kate Moss. Claire Lippman, though, who's gotta be thirty-four, twenty-four, thirty-eight or so, they drool over. I think a lot of it is how you project yourself, and Claire Lippman projects herself like she's got it on, you know?

Ruth doesn't. Project herself with any confidence, I mean. Ruth's problem is that she's just, you know, a big girl. All the crash diets in the world aren't going to change that. She just needs to accept that and accept herself and calm down. Then she'll get a boyfriend. Guaranteed.

But probably not Mike.

I was thinking about how weird bodies are while I poured myself a bowl of cereal. I wondered if the star-shaped scar was going to stay on my chest. I mean, who needed that? And where was that exit wound, anyway?

Maybe, I thought, as I poured milk over my Total with raisins, the lightning was still inside of me. That would have been weird, huh? Maybe I was walking around with it buzzing inside of me. And maybe, like Ruth said, I could send it shooting at people. Like Jeff Day. He so deserved it. I thought about shooting bolts of lightning at Jeff Day while I read the back of the milk carton. Man, would that put a crimp in his football career.

When I got back upstairs, Ruth was gone. Mike's door was closed, but I knew she wasn't in there, because I heard him typing furiously on his computer. Probably sending E-mail to all his dweeby Internet buddies. Hey, guys, I got into Harvard! Just like Bill Gates.

Only maybe, unlike Bill Gates, Mike would actually graduate. Not that that had mattered, at least in Bill's case.

The door to Douglas's room was closed, too, and no light spilled out from under it. But that didn't stop me. Douglas was at his window, a pair of binoculars to his head, when I came barging in.

He turned around and went, "One of these days, you're going to do that and you're going to end up seeing something you really never wanted to see."

"Already saw it," I said. "Mom used to make us take baths together when we were little, remember?"

He said, "Go away. I'm busy."

"What are you looking at, anyway?" I asked, going to sit on his bed in the darkness. Douglas's room smelled like Douglas. Not a bad smell, really. Just a boy smell. Like old sneakers mingled with Old Spice. "Claire Lippman?"

"Orion," he said, but I knew he was lying. His room has a view straight into Claire Lippman's, two houses away. Claire, exhibitionist that she is, never pulls down her blinds. I doubt she even has blinds.

But I didn't mind Douglas spying on her, even though it was sexist and a violation of her privacy and all. It meant he was normal. Well, for him, anyway.

"Not to tear you away from your lady love," I said, "but I found an entrance wound."

"She's not my lady love," Douglas said. "Merely the object of my lust."

"Well, whatever," I said. I pulled on the neck of my sweatshirt. "Take a look at this."

He turned on his reading lamp and swiveled it in my direction. When he saw the scar, he got real quiet.

"Jesus Christ," he said after a while.

"Told you," I said.

He said, "Jesus Christ," again.

"There's no exit wound," I said. "I had Ruth check me, all over. Nothing. Do you think the lightning is still inside me?"

"Lightning," he said, "does not just stay inside

you. Maybe this is the exit wound, and the bolt came in through the top of your head. Only that isn't possible," he said, to himself, I guess, "because then her hair would be scorched."

It was possible, though, that he wasn't speaking to himself. He could have been speaking to the voices. He hears voices sometimes. They were the ones who told him to kill himself last Christmas.

"Well," I said, letting my sweatshirt snap back into place. "That's all. I just wanted to show you."

"Wait a minute." I had gotten up, but Douglas pulled me back down onto his bed again. "Jess," he said. "Did you *really* get struck by lightning?"

"*Yes,*" I said. "I *told* you I did."

Douglas looked serious. But then, Douglas was always serious. "You should tell Dad."

"No way."

"I mean it, Jess. Go tell Dad, right now. Not Mom, either. Just Dad."

"Aw, Douglas . . ."

"Go." He pulled me up and pushed me toward the door. "Either you do it, or I will."

"Aw, hell," I said.

But he started to look funny, all pinch-faced and stuff. So I dragged myself downstairs and found my dad where he usually was when he wasn't at one of the restaurants—at the dining room table, going over the books, with the TV in the kitchen turned to the sports channel. He couldn't see the TV from where he sat, but he could hear it. Even though he looked totally absorbed in the numbers in front of him, if you switched the channel, he'd totally freak out.

"What," he said when I came in. But not in an unfriendly way.

"Hey, Dad," I said. "Douglas says I have to tell you I got hit by lightning today."

My dad looked up. He had his reading glasses on. He looked at me over the tops of them.

"Is Douglas having an episode?" he asked. That's what the shrinks call it when Douglas's voices get the better of him. An episode.

"No," I said. "It's really true. I did get struck by lightning today."

He looked at me some more. "Why didn't you mention this at dinner?"

"Because, you know," I said, "it was a celebration. But Douglas said I have to tell you. Ruth, too. She says I could have a heart attack in my sleep. See, look."

I stretched out the neck of my sweatshirt again. It was okay, because the scar was way above my boobs, up by my collarbone. My dad's been kind of weird about my boobs, ever since I got some. I think he's afraid they'll get in the way of my swing when I haul off a right hook at somebody.

He looked at the scar and went, "Were you and Skip playing with firecrackers again?"

I think I mentioned before that Skip is Ruth's

twin brother. He and I used to have a thing about firecrackers.

"No, Dad," I said. "Jeez. I'm way over firecrackers." Not to mention Skip. "That's from the lightning."

I told him what had happened. He listened with this very serious look on his face. Then he went, "I wouldn't worry about it."

That's what he always used to say when I'd wake up in what seemed like the middle of the night—but was probably only about eleven—when I was a very little kid, and I'd come down and tell him my leg, or my arm, or my neck hurt.

"Growing pains," he'd say, and give me a glass of milk. "I wouldn't worry about it."

"Okay," I said. I was just as relieved as I'd been back then, when I was little. "I just thought I should tell you. You know, in case I don't wake up tomorrow morning."

He said, "You don't wake up tomorrow, your mother will kill you. Now go to bed. And if I hear anything about you seeking shelter under metal again during a thunderstorm, I'll wear you out."

He didn't mean it, of course. My dad doesn't believe in spanking. That's because his older brother, my uncle Rick, used to beat the tar out of him, my mom says. Which is why we never go to visit Uncle Rick. I think that's also why my dad taught me how to punch. My dad thinks you have to learn to defend yourself from all the Uncle Ricks of the world.

I went back upstairs and practiced my flute for an hour. I always try to play my best when I practice ever since this one morning, back before Ruth got her car and we used to take the bus to school, Claire Lippman saw me with my flute case, and went, "Oh, you're the one," in this meaningful voice. When I asked her what she meant, she said, "Oh, nothing. Just that we always hear someone playing the flute around ten o'clock every night, and we never knew who it was." So I was totally mortified and turned bright red, which she must have seen, since she went, in this nice voice—Claire, in spite of being an exhibitionist, is really pretty nice—"No, no, it's not bad. I like it. It's like a free concert every night."

Anyway, once I heard that, I started treating my practice hour like a performance. First I warm up with scales, but I do them really fast to get them over with, and kind of jazzy, so that they don't sound boring. Then I work on whatever we're doing in Orchestra, but at double-time, also to get it over with. Then I do some cool medieval pieces I dug up last time I went to the library, some really ancient versions of *Greensleeves* and some Celtic stuff. Then, when I'm totally warmed up, I do some Billy Joel, since that's Douglas's favorite, though he'd deny it if you asked him. Then I do some Gershwin, for my dad, who loves Gershwin, and finish up with some Bach, because who doesn't love Bach?

Sometimes Ruth and I will practice together on the few pieces we've found for flute and cello. But we don't practice from the same house. What we do is, we open our bedroom windows and play from there. Like a little mini-concert for the neighborhood. That's pretty cool. Ruth says if some conductor walked by our houses, he'd be like, "Who are those incredible musicians? I need them in my orchestra immediately!" She's probably right.

The thing is, I play much better at home than I do at school. Like, if I played as well at school as I do at home, I'd definitely be first chair, instead of third. But I mess up a lot at school on purpose, because, frankly, I don't want to be first chair. First chair is way too much pressure. I get enough grief as it is from people trying to challenge me for third.

Karen Sue Hanky, for instance. She's fourth chair. She's challenged me ten times already this year. If you don't like your chair, you can challenge the person ahead of you, and move up if you win. Karen Sue started out as ninth chair, and challenged her way up to fourth. But she's been stuck at fourth all year, because one thing I won't do is let her win. I like third chair. I'm always third chair. Third chair, third kid. You get it? I'm comfortable being third.

But no way am I going to be fourth. So whenever Karen Sue challenges me, I play my best, like I do at home. Our conductor, Mr. Vine, always gives me this lecture afterward, when Karen Sue's gone off in a huff, which she always does, because I always win. Then Mr. Vine goes, "You know, Jessica, you could be first chair, if you'd just challenge Audrey. You could blow Audrey away, if you just tried."

But I have no desire to blow anybody away. I don't want to be first chair, or even second chair.

But I'll be damned before I let anybody take third chair away from me.

Anyway, when I was done practicing, I took a shower, and then went to bed. Before I turned out the light, though, I felt the place on my chest where the scar was. I couldn't really feel it. It wasn't raised, or anything. But I could still see it, when I'd looked in the mirror coming out of the shower. I hoped it wouldn't still be there the next day. How else was I going to wear my scoop-necked T-shirt?

CHAPTER

5

When I woke up the next morning, I knew two things right away. One, I had not died of a heart attack in the night. And two, Sean Patrick O'Hanahan was in Paoli, while Olivia Marie D'Amato was in New Jersey.

That's three things, I guess. But the second two were totally random. Who the hell was Sean Patrick O'Hanahan, and how did I know he was in Paoli? Ditto the stuff about Olivia Marie D'Amato.

Crazy dreams. I'd been having some crazy dreams, that was all. I got up and took another shower, since the red mark was still there, and I couldn't wear the scoop neck. I decided to go for clean hair instead. Who knew? Maybe Rob Wilkins would offer me another ride, and when we were at a stop sign or something, he'd turn his head and smell me.

It could happen.

It wasn't until I was eating breakfast that I realized who Sean Patrick O'Hanahan and Olivia Marie D'Amato were. They were the kids on the back of the milk carton. You know, the missing ones. Only they weren't missing. Not anymore. Because I knew where they were.

"You don't think you're actually wearing those jeans to school, do you, Jessica?"

My mom was way disenchanted with my ensemble, which I had put together very carefully, with Rob Wilkins in mind.

"Yeah, really," Mike said. "What do you think this is? The eighties?"

"Like," I said, "you know anything about fashion, science boy. Where's your pocket protector, anyway?"

"You cannot," my mother said, "wear those jeans to school, Jessica. You'll shame the family."

"There's nothing wrong with my jeans," I said. 1-800-WHERE-R-YOU. That was the number you were supposed to call if you knew where Sean Patrick O'Hanahan or Olivia Marie D'Amato were. I'm not kidding. 1-800-WHERE-R-YOU. Cute. Very cute.

"The knees have given out," my mother went on. "There's a hole starting at the crotch. You can't wear those jeans. They're falling apart."

That was the point, see. I couldn't expose my chest area, so I'd decided to go for my knees. I have pretty nice knees. So, when I was riding behind Rob Wilkins on his motorcycle, he'd look down and see these totally sexy knees sticking out of my jeans. I'd shaved my legs and everything. I was way ready.

The one thing I hadn't figured out was how I was going to get a ride home if he didn't ask. Call Ruth, I guess. But Ruth was going to be mad at me if I asked her not to come in the first place. She was bound to be all, "Why? Who's taking you home? Not that Grit, I hope."

Being best friends with someone like Ruth is hard sometimes.

"Go upstairs and change, young lady," my mom said.

"No way." My mouth was filled with cereal.

"What do you mean, no way? You cannot go to school dressed like that."

"Watch me," I said.

My dad came in then. My mom went, "Joe, look what she's wearing."

"What?" I said. "They're just jeans."

My dad looked at my jeans. Then he looked at my mom. "They're just jeans, Toni," he said.

My mom's name is Antonia. Everyone calls her Toni.

"They're slut jeans," my mother said. "She's dressing in slut jeans. It's because she reads that slut magazine." That's what my mom calls *Cosmo*. It sort of *is* a slut magazine, but still.

"She doesn't look like a slut," my dad said. "She just looks like what she is." We all looked at him questioningly, wondering what I was. Then he went, "Well, you know. A tomboy."

Fortunately, at that moment, Ruth honked outside.

"Okay," I said, getting up. "I gotta go."

"Not in those jeans, you're not," my mom said.

I grabbed my flute and my backpack. "Bye," I said, and left by the back door.

I ran all the way around to the front of the house to meet Ruth, who was waiting in the street in her Cabriolet. It was a nice morning, so she had the top down.

"Nice jeans," she said sarcastically, as I climbed into the passenger seat.

"Just drive," I said.

"Really," she said, shifting. "You don't look like Jennifer Beals, or anything. Hey, are you a welder by day and a stripper by night, by any chance?"

"Yes," I said. "But I'm saving all my money to pay for ballet school."

We were almost to school when Ruth asked, suddenly, "Hey, what's with you? You haven't been this quiet since Douglas tried to . . . you know."

I shook myself. I hadn't been aware of vegging, but that's exactly what I'd done. The thing was, I couldn't get this picture of Sean Patrick O'Hanahan out of my head. He was older in my dream than in the picture on the milk carton.

Maybe he was one of those kids who'd been kidnapped so long ago, he didn't remember his real
family.

Then again, maybe it had just been a dream.

"Huh," I said. "I don't know. I was just thinking, is all."

"That's a first," Ruth said. She pulled into the
student parking lot. "Hey, do you want to walk
home again tonight? I'll have Skip drop me off
again at four, when you get out of detention. You
know, I weighed myself this morning, and I
already lost a pound."

I think she probably lost the pound from not
eating any dinner the night before, being way too
busy staring dreamily at Mike to consume anything. But all I said was, "Sure, I guess.
Except . . ."

"Except what?"

"Well, you know how I feel about motorcycles."

Ruth looked heavenward. "Not Rob Wilkins
again."

"Yes, Rob Wilkins again. I can't help it, Ruth.
He's got that really big—"

"I don't want to hear it," Ruth said, holding
up her hand.

"—Indian," I finished. "What did you think I
was going to say?"

"I don't know." Ruth pushed a button, and the
roof started going up. "Some of those Grits wear
pretty tight jeans."

"Gross," I said, as if this had never occurred to me. "Really, Ruth."

She undid her seatbelt primly. "Well, it's not like I'm blind or anything."

"Look," I said. "If he offers me a ride, I'm taking it."

"It's your life," Ruth said. "But don't expect me to sit by the phone waiting for you to call if he doesn't ask."

"If he doesn't ask," I said, "I'll just call my mom."

"Fine," Ruth said. She sounded mad.

"What?"

"Nothing," she said.

"No, not nothing. What's wrong?"

"Nothing's wrong." Ruth got out of the car. "God, you're such a weirdo."

Ruth is always calling me a weirdo, so I didn't take offense. I don't think she even means anything by it anymore. Anything much, anyway.

I got out of the car, too. It was a beautiful day, the sky a robin's-egg blue overhead, the temperature hovering around sixty, and it was only eight in the morning. The afternoon would probably be roasting. Not the kind of day to spend indoors. The perfect kind of day for a ride in a convertible . . . or, even better, on the back of a bike.

Which reminded me. Paoli was only about twenty miles from where I was standing. It was the next town over, actually. I couldn't help won-

dering how Ruth—or Rob Wilkins—would feel
about taking a little trip over there after detention. You know, just to check it out. I wouldn't
tell either of them about my dream or anything.
But I was pretty sure I knew exactly where that
little brick house was . . . even though I was
equally sure I'd never been there before.

Which was the main reason, actually, that I
wanted to check it out. I mean, who goes around
having dreams about kids on the back of milk
cartons? Not that my ordinary dreams are all that
exciting. Just the usual ones, about showing up
to school naked, or sucking face with Brendan
Fraser.

"Hello?"

I blinked. Ruth was standing in front of me,
waving a hand in my face.

"God," she said, putting her hand down.
"What is the matter with you? Are you sure
you're all right?"

"Fine," I said automatically.

And the funny thing was, I really thought I
was fine.

Then.

CHAPTER

6

Detention at Ernie Pyle High is traditionally run by the staff member with the least seniority. This year, it was Miss Clemmings, the new art teacher. Now, I don't mean to be sexist, but they had to be kidding. Miss Clemmings is barely as tall as me, and can't weigh more than I do, like a hundred pounds or so.

And yet, unlike me, Miss Clemmings is hardly an expert kickboxer—or even a mediocre one. But there she was, supposed to keep these giant football players from fighting with one another. I mean, it was ridiculous. Coach Albright I could see. Coach Albright would be able to establish some control. But all Miss Clemmings could do was threaten to report these guys when they acted up. And all that happened when they got reported was that they got longer detentions.

Miss Clemmings had to keep them from fighting that much longer. It was kind of retarded.

So I wasn't super-surprised when Miss Clemmings, at the start of detention at the end of the day, called me up to the front of the auditorium and said, in her wispy little-girl voice, "Jessica, I need to talk to you."

I couldn't imagine what Miss Clemmings wanted. Oh, all right, I'll admit it: a part of me thought she was going to let me off for the rest of the semester, on account of my good behavior. Because I really am a little angel . . . during detention, anyway. That was more than could be said for any of my fellow detainees.

Which was, in a way, what she wanted to talk to me about.

"It's the *W*s," she whispered.

I looked at her uncomprehendingly. "The *W*s, Miss Clemmings?"

She went, "Yes, in the back row?" And then she pointed at the auditorium seats.

It was only then that I caught on. Of course. The *W*s. We're seated alphabetically for detention, and the guys in the last row—the *W*s—have a tendency to get a little rambunctious. They'd been restless during rehearsals for *West Side Story*, rowdy during *Romeo and Juliet*, and downright rude during *Our Town.* Now the drama club was putting on *Endgame*, and Miss Clemmings was afraid a riot might break out.

"I hate to ask this of you, Jessica," she said,

looking at me with her big blue eyes, "but you are the only girl here, and I've often found that placing a strong female influence in amongst a predominantly testosterone-driven group has a tendency to diffuse some of the—"

"Okay," I said, real fast.

Miss Clemmings looked surprised. Then she looked relieved. "Really? Really, Jessica? You wouldn't mind?"

Was she kidding? "No," I said. "I wouldn't mind. Not at all."

"Oh," she said, placing a hand to her heart. "Oh, I'm so glad. If you could, then, just sit between Robert Wilkins and the Wendell boy—"

I couldn't believe it. Some days, you know, you wake up, and okay, maybe you had some wacked-out dreams, but then, suddenly, things just start going your way. Just like that.

I went back to my seat in the Ms, picked up my backpack and my flute, and shoved my way down the W row until I'd gotten to the seat between Rob and Hank. There were a lot of cat-calls while I did this—enough so that the drama coach turned around and shushed us—and a few of the guys wouldn't pick up their stupid feet and let me by. I got them back, however, by kicking them really hard in the shins. That got them moving, all right.

We have to sit one seat apart from one another, so that necessitated everyone from Rob Wilkins down moving one seat over. Only Rob didn't

seem to mind. He picked up his leather jacket—
he had nothing else, no books, no bag, nothing,
except a paperback spy novel he kept in the back
pocket of his jeans—and sat down again, his blue
eyes on me as I arranged my stuff under my seat.

"Welcome to hell," he said to me when I
straightened up.

I flashed him my best smile. The guy on the
other side of him saw it, and grabbed his crotch.
Rob noticed, looked at him, and said, "You're
dead, Wylie."

"Shhh," Miss Clemmings hissed, clapping her
hands at us. "If I hear another word back there,
you're all getting an extra week."

We shut up. I took out my geometry book and
started doing the homework we'd been assigned
for the weekend. I tried not to notice that Rob
wasn't doing anything. He was just sitting there,
watching the play rehearsal. The guy to my left,
Hank Wendell, was making one of those paper
footballs. He was using spit instead of tape to
hold the paper together.

None of the guys in the Ws seemed particularly impressed—or cowed—by my presence.

Then suddenly Rob leaned over and grabbed
my notebook and pen out of my hands. He
looked at my homework, nodded, and turned the
page. Then he wrote something down, and
passed the notebook and the pen back to me. I
looked at what he had written. It was:

So did you get caught in the rain yesterday?

I looked down at Miss Clemmings. I'm not sure whether or not you're allowed to pass notes in detention. I'd never heard of anybody trying it before.

But Miss Clemmings wasn't even paying attention. She was watching Claire Lippman perform this really boring monologue from inside a big Rubbermaid trash can.

I wrote, *Yes*, and passed the notebook back to him.

Not exactly scintillating, or anything. But what else was I supposed to say?

He wrote something down and passed the notebook back. He'd written: *Told you so. Why don't you ditch the fat girl and come for a ride with me after this?*

Jesus Christ. He was asking me out. Sort of.

And he was also dissing my best friend.

Are you mentally impaired or something? I wrote. *That fat girl happens to be my best friend.*

He seemed to like that. He wrote for a long time. When I got the notebook back, this is what he'd put down: *Jesus, sorry. I had no idea you were so sensitive. Let me rephrase. Why don't you tell your gravitationally challenged friend to take a hike, and come for a ride with me after this?*

I wrote: *It's Friday night, you loser. What do you think, I don't already have plans? I happen to have a boyfriend, you know.*

I thought the boyfriend part might be stretching it a little, but he seemed to eat it up. He wrote: *Yeah? Well, I bet your boyfriend isn't rebuilding a '64 Harley in his barn.*

A '64 Harley? My fingers were trembling so hard I could barely write. *My boyfriend doesn't have a barn. His dad*—as long as I was making up a boyfriend, I figured I'd give him an impressive lineage—*is a lawyer.*

Rob wrote: *So? Dump him. Come for a ride.*

It was right then that Hank Wendell leaned over and went, "Wylie. Wylie?"

On the other side of Rob, Greg Wylie leaned over and went, "Suck on this, Wendell."

"Both of you," I hissed through gritted teeth, "shut the hell up before Clemmings looks over here."

Hank sent his paper football flying in Wylie's direction. But Rob stuck out his hand and caught it before it got to where it was supposed to.

"You heard the lady," he said, in this dangerous voice. "Knock it off."

Both Wylie and Wendell simmered down. Boy. Miss Clemmings had been right. It was amazing what a little estrogen could do.

Okay, I wrote. *On one condition.*

He wrote, *No conditions* and underlined it heavily.

I wrote, in big block letters, *Then I can't go.*

He'd seen what I was writing before I finished it. He snatched the notebook from me, looking annoyed, and wrote, *All right. What?*

Which was how, an hour later, we were headed for Paoli.

CHAPTER

7

Okay. Okay, so I'll admit it. Right here, on paper, in my official *statement.* You want a confession? You want me to tell the truth?

Okay. Here it is:

I like to go fast.

I mean, *really* fast.

I don't know what it is. I've just never been scared of speed. On road trips, like when we'd drive up to Chicago to see Grandma, and my dad would go eighty or so, trying to pass a semi, everyone in the car would be like, "Slow down! Slow down!"

Not me. I was always, "Faster! Faster!"

It's been that way ever since I was a little girl. I remember back when we used go to the county fair (before it was determined to be too "Gritty"), I always had to go on all the fast rides—the

Whip, the Super Himalaya—by myself, because everyone else in my family was too scared of them. Just me, by myself, going sixty, seventy, eighty miles an hour.

And that still wasn't fast enough. Not for me.

But here's the thing I found out that day I went for a ride with Rob: Rob liked going fast, too.

He was safe about it and everything. Like he made me wear a spare helmet he had in the storage container on the back of the bike. And he obeyed all traffic laws, while we were still within city limits. But as soon as we were out of them . . .

I have to tell you, I was in heaven. I mean it.

Of course, part of it might have been because I had my arms wrapped around this totally buff guy. I mean, Rob had abs that were hard as rock. I know, because I was holding on pretty tight, and all he was wearing beneath that leather jacket was a T-shirt.

Rob was my kind of guy. He liked taking risks.

It wasn't like there were any other cars on the road. I mean, we're talking country lanes here, surrounded by corn fields. I don't think we passed another car all night, except when we finally made the turn into Paoli.

Paoli.

What can I tell you about Paoli? What do you want to know? You want to know how it started? I guess you do. Okay, I'll tell you. It started in Paoli.

Paoli, Indiana. Paoli's just like any other small town in Southern Indiana. There was a town square with a courthouse on it, one movie theater, a bridal shop, a library. I guess there was probably an elementary school, too, and a high school, and a rubber tire factory, though I didn't see them.

I do know there were about ten churches. I made Rob turn left at one of the churches—don't even ask me how I knew it was the right one— and suddenly we were on the same tree-lined street from my dream. Two blocks later, and we were in front of this very familiar-looking little brick house. I tapped Rob on the shoulder, and he pulled over to the curb and cut the engine off.

Then we sat there, and I looked.

It was the house from my dream. The exact same house. It had the same crabgrassy lawn, the same black mailbox with just numbers, no name on it, the same windows with all the blinds down. The more I looked at it, the more I suspected that, in the backyard, there'd be a rusty old swing set, and one of those kiddie wading pools, cracked and dirty from having sat outside all winter.

It was a nice house. Small, but nice. In a modest but nice neighborhood. Someone who lived nearby had gotten out the barbecue and was grilling burgers for dinner. In the distance, I could hear the voices of children shouting as they played.

"Well," Rob said, after a minute. "This the boyfriend's place, then?"

"Shhh," I said to him. That's because someone was coming toward us on the sidewalk. Someone short, dragging a jean jacket behind him. Someone who, when he got close enough, suddenly veered off the sidewalk and onto the lawn of the little brick house I was staring at.

I pulled off the helmet Rob had lent me.

No, my eyes weren't playing tricks on me. It was Sean Patrick O'Hanahan, all right. Older than he'd been in the picture on the back of the milk carton by about five or six years. But it was him. I just knew it.

I don't know what made me do it. I'd never done anything like it before. But I got down from Rob's bike, crossed the street, and said, "Sean."

Just like that. I didn't yell it or anything. I just said his name.

He turned. Then he went pale. Before he even saw me, he went pale. I swear it.

He was probably about twelve. Small for his age, but still only a few inches shorter than me. Red hair beneath a Yankees cap. Freckles stood out starkly against his nose, now that he'd gone so pale.

His eyes were blue. They narrowed as his gaze flicked first over me, then behind me, toward Rob.

"I don't know what you're talking about," he said. He didn't shout it, any more than I'd shouted his name. Still, I heard the undercurrent of fear in his little-boy voice.

I got as far as the sidewalk before I thought I'd better stop. He looked ready to bolt.

"Oh, yeah?" I said. "Your name's not Sean?"

"No," the kid said, in that snotty way kids talk when they're scared, only they don't want it to show. "My name's Sam."

I shook my head slowly. "No, it isn't," I said. "Your name's Sean. Sean Patrick O'Hanahan. It's okay, Sean. You can trust me. I'm here to help you. I'm here to help get you home."

What happened next was this:

The kid went, if such a thing is possible, even whiter. At the same time, his body seemed to turn into Jell-O, or something. He dropped the jean jacket as if it weighed too much for him to hold on to anymore, and I could see his fingers shaking.

Then he rushed me.

I don't know what I thought he was going to do. Hug me, I guess. I thought maybe he was so happy and grateful at being found, he was going to throw himself into my arms and give me a great big kiss for having come to his rescue.

That was so not what he did.

What he did instead was reach out and grab me by the wrist—quite painfully, I might add—and hiss, *"Don't you tell anyone. Don't you ever tell anyone you saw me, understand?"*

This was not exactly the kind of reaction I'd

been expecting. I mean, it would have been one thing if we'd gotten to Paoli and I had found out the house I'd dreamed about didn't exist. But it did exist. And what's more, in front of that house was the kid from the milk carton. I'd have staked my life on it.

Only, for some reason, the kid was claiming he was someone else.

"I am not Sean Patrick O'Hanahan," he whispered in a voice that was as filled with anger as it was with fear. "So you can just go away, do you hear? You can just go away. *And don't ever come back.*"

It was at this point that the front door to the little house opened, and a woman's voice called, sharply, "Sam!"

The kid let go of me at once.

"Coming," he said, his voice shaking as badly as his fingers were.

He threw me just one more furious, frightened look as he stooped to pick his jean jacket up off the lawn. Then he ran inside and slammed the door behind him without glancing in my direction again.

Standing out on the sidewalk, I stared at that closed door. I listened to the sounds of the birds, of the children I could hear playing somewhere nearby. I could still smell the burgers grilling, and something else: fresh-cut grass. Someone had taken advantage of the unseasonable warmth and mowed their lawn.

Nothing inside the house in front of me stirred. Not a blind was lifted. Nothing.

But everything—everything I had ever known—was different now.

Because that kid *was* Sean Patrick O'Hanahan. I knew it as well as I knew my name, my brothers' names. That kid was Sean Patrick O'Hanahan.

And he was in trouble.

"Kid's a little young for you," I heard a voice behind me point out, "don't you think?"

I turned around. Rob was still straddling the motorcycle. He'd taken his helmet off, and was observing me with a perfectly impassive expression on his good-looking face.

"Takes all kinds, I guess," he said with a shrug. "Still, I didn't have you pegged for having a Boy Scout fixation."

I probably should have told him. I probably should have said right then, *Look, I saw that kid on the back of a milk carton. Let's go get the police.*

But I didn't. I didn't say anything. I didn't know what to say. I didn't know what to do.

I didn't understand what was happening to me.

"Well," Rob said. "We could stand around out here all night, if you want to. But the smell of those burgers is making me hungry. What do you say we go try to find some of our own?"

I gave the little brick house one last look. *Sean,* I thought to myself, *I know that's you in there. What did they do to you? What did they do to you, to make you so afraid to admit your own name?*

"Mastriani," Rob said.

I turned around and got back onto the bike.

He didn't ask me a single question. He just handed me my helmet, put his own on, waited until I said I was ready, and then he hit the gas.

We left Paoli.

It wasn't until we were doing ninety again that I perked up. It's hard to keep a speed freak down when she's doing ninety. Okay, I reasoned to myself as we cruised. You know what you have to do. You know what you have to do.

So after we'd pulled up to the burger place Rob had in mind—a Hell's Angels hangout called Chick's that I'd always wanted to go to, since we drove past it every January 5 on our way to the dump to get rid of the Christmas tree, only Mom would never let me—I did it.

I went to the pay phone by the ladies' room and dialed.

"1-800-WHERE-R-YOU," a woman's voice said after it had only rung twice. "This is Rosemary. How may I help you?"

I had to stick a finger in my other ear, the juke-box was pumping John Cougar Mellencamp so loudly.

"Hi, Rosemary," I shouted. "This is Jess."

"Hi, Jess," Rosemary said. She sounded like she might be black. I don't happen to know any black people—there aren't any in my town—but I have seen them in movies, and on TV and stuff. So that's how I knew. Rosemary sounded

like an older black lady. "I can barely hear
you."

"Yeah," I said. "Sorry about that. I'm in a . . .
well, I'm in a bar."

Rosemary didn't sound too shaken to hear
that. On the other hand, she had no way of
knowing that I am only sixteen.

"What can I do for you today, Jess?" Rosemary
asked.

"Well," I said. I took a deep breath.

"Listen, Rosemary," I said. "This is going to
sound kind of weird, but there's this kid, Sean
Patrick O'Hanahan. You guys have him on a milk
carton. Anyway, I know where he is." And then I
told her.

Rosemary kept going, "Uh-huh. Uh-huh. Uh-
huh." And then she said, "Honey, are you—"

Rob shouted my name. I looked toward him,
and he held up two red plastic baskets. Our burgers were up.

I went, "Rosemary, I gotta go. But real quick.
That Olivia Marie D'Amato? You guys'll be able
to find her at—" And then I gave her a street
address, a city in New Jersey, and a zip code, for
good measure. "Okay? I gotta go. Bye!"

I hung up.

It was funny, but I felt relieved. Like I had gotten something off my chest. Isn't that weird? I
mean, I know Sean had told me not to tell anyone.

Told me not to tell? He'd *begged* me.

But he had also looked so scared at being

found out that I couldn't imagine whoever he was with could be any good for him. Not if they were making him lie about his name and stuff. What about his parents? He had to know they were missing him. He had to know they would protect him from whoever these people were who had him.

I had done the right thing, calling. I had to have. Otherwise, why would I have felt so good?

I ended up having a good time. Rob, it turned out, had quite a few friends at Chick's. All of them were guys who were way older than he was, and, for the most part, they had really long hair and were heavily tattooed. Their tattoos said things like *1/31/68*, which I remembered from World Civ was the day of the Tet Offensive in the Vietnam war. Rob's friends seemed strangely astonished to see me—although they were very nice—which led me to believe that either:

a) Rob had never brought a girl to Chick's before (unlikely), or
b) the girls he'd brought there had looked more like the girls who were hanging around the Hell's Angels—i.e., tall, blond, excessively made-up, named Teri or Charleen, and who probably never wore gingham in their lives (more likely).

Which might be why, every time I opened my mouth, the guys would all look at one another, until finally one of them said to Rob, "Where'd you *get* her?" to which I replied, because it was such a stupid question, "The girlfriend store."

Everybody but Teri and Charleen laughed at that one.

So, overall, when I got home that night, I was one happy camper. I had saved a kid's life—maybe even two kids' lives, although there was no way I was going all the way to Jersey to check Olivia D'Amato's situation. And I had spent the afternoon and part of the evening with a totally hot guy who liked going fast, and who, if I wasn't mistaken, seemed to like me, too. What could be better than that?

Not having my parents find out about it, that's what.

And there was no chance they were going to, either. Because the minute I walked in the door, around nine or so—I made Rob drop me off way down the street, so my folks wouldn't hear his bike—I saw that they hadn't even noticed I was gone. I had called, of course, from Chick's, and said band rehearsal was running long, but nobody had picked up. When I walked in, I saw why. My mom and dad were having a huge fight. Over Douglas. As usual.

"He's not ready!" my mom was screaming.

"The longer he waits," my dad said, "the harder it's going to be for him. He's got to start now."

"Do you want him to try it again?" my mom wanted to know. "Is that what you want, Joe?"

"Of course not," my dad said. "But it's different now. He's on the medication. Look, Toni, I think it would be good for him. He needs to get out of the house. All he does is lie up there, reading comic books."

"And you think slaving away in a hot restaurant kitchen is the cure for that?" My mom sounded very sarcastic.

"He needs to get out," my dad said. "And he needs to start earning his keep."

"He's sick!" my mom insisted.

"He's always going to be sick, Toni," my dad said. "But at least he's being treated now. And the treatments are working. The doctors said as long as he was taking his medication, there's no reason why he can't—" My dad broke off because he saw me in the doorway. "What do you want?" he asked, not rudely.

"Cereal," I said. "Sorry I missed dinner."

My dad waved at me. A *whatever* wave. I got down a box of Raisin Bran and a bowl.

"He's not ready," my mother said.

"Toni," my dad said. "He can't stay up there in his room forever. I mean, he's twenty years old, for Christ's sake. He's got to start getting out, seeing people his own age—"

"Oh, and back in the kitchen at Mastriani's, that's what he'll be doing. Getting out." My mom was being sarcastic again.

"Yes," my dad said. "With kids his own age. You know the crew back there. They'll be good for him."

My mother snorted. I ate my cereal, pretending to be very interested in the back of the milk carton, but really listening to their conversation.

"Next thing, you'll probably want to send him to one of those halfway houses," my mother said.

"Well, Toni," my dad said, "it might not be such a bad idea. He could meet other kids with his same problem, learn he's not alone in this—"

"I don't like it," my mother said. "I'm telling you, I don't like it."

My dad threw his hands in the air. "Of course you don't like it, Toni," he said. "You want to keep the kid wrapped up in cotton wool. But you can't do it, Toni. You can't protect him forever. And you can't watch him forever. He's going to find a way to do it again, whether you're keeping an eye on him or not."

"Dad's right," I said with my mouth full.

My mother glared at me. "Don't you have some place to be, young lady?"

I didn't, but I decided to go to my room to practice. Nobody bothered asking me why I was practicing after I'd just—supposedly—been at band practice for like six hours or something. That's just the way my family is.

Claire Lippman's not the only one who can hear me practicing. Ruth can hear me, too. As soon as I was done, the phone rang. It was Ruth, wanting to know all about my bike ride.

"It was okay," I said as I ran a cloth through

the inside of my flute with this metal stick to clean out all the spit.

"Okay?" Ruth echoed. *"Okay?* What'd you do? Where did you go?"

"Just for a ride," I said. Don't ask me why, but I couldn't bring myself to tell Ruth about Sean. I hadn't even been able to tell Rob about Sean. In answer to his persistent questioning, I'd finally said, "He's my loan shark, okay?" which had gotten a hoot from Rob's friends.

"You went for a ride?" Ruth's voice rose incredulously. "To where? Chicago?"

"No. Just around. And then we went to Chick's."

"Chick's?" Ruth sounded close to sponta-neous combustion. "That's a *bar.* A *biker* bar."

"Yeah," I said.

"And you didn't get carded?"

"No," I said. We didn't get carded because Rob knew the bartender.

"Did you *drink?"*

"Of course not," I said.

"Did he?"

"Duh, Ruth. Do you think I really would have gotten onto a bike with a guy who was drinking? We just had sodas."

"Oh. Well, did he kiss you?"

I didn't say anything. I was taking my flute apart, putting it into the little velvet compart-ments inside my case.

"Jeez," Ruth breathed. "He did. I can't believe he kissed you. Was there tongue?"

"Regrettably, no."

"Oh, my God," Ruth said. "Well, that's probably better. You shouldn't let him tongue you on a first date. He might think you're easy. So, are you going out again?"

"Maybe next weekend," I said, vaguely. He hadn't mentioned a thing, I realized now, about seeing me again. What did *that* mean? Did he not like me? Or was it just that it was my turn to ask him? Never having dated before, I was not sure how these things worked.

And there was no use asking Ruth. She was even more clueless than I was.

"I still can't believe," she was saying, "that you're seeing a Grit."

"You're such a snob," I said. "What does it matter? He's totally cool. And he knows everything about bikes."

"But he's not going to college, right? After he graduates?"

"No. He's going to work in his uncle's garage."

"Jeez," Ruth said. "Well, I guess it's okay if you just use him for sex and free bike rides."

"I'm hanging up now, Ruth," I said.

"Okay. You working tomorrow?"

"Is the Pope Catholic?"

"Okay. Wow. I can't believe he kissed you."

Actually, I couldn't, either. But I didn't tell

Ruth that. Or about how, when he'd done it, I'd practically fallen off the back of his bike, I'd been so surprised. Just because I'm in detention a lot doesn't mean I'm experienced.

I hope it didn't show.

CHAPTER

8

Every Saturday, and most Sundays after church, I have to work at one of my dad's restaurants. So does Michael. So did Douglas, before he went away to college, and got sick. I guess all kids whose parents own restaurants have to work in them at some point. It's supposed to teach us to have a work ethic, so we don't go around thinking everything just gets handed to you on a platter. Instead, we're the ones handling the platter. And the dishes. And the steam table. And the cash register. And the reservation book.

You name it, and if it has to do with food service, I've done it.

That particular Saturday, though, I was kind of spacing it with the cash register, so Pat, the manager, stuck me on busing. Hey, I had a lot on my mind. And no, it wasn't Rob Wilkins. It was the fact that, when I'd woken up that morning, I knew where Hadley Grant and Timothy Jonas Mills were.

My mom had thrown out the old milk carton, the one with Sean Patrick and Olivia Marie, and bought a new one. And I knew where the missing kids on the new one were, too.

It was freaking me out a little. I mean, where were these dreams coming from? It was so random to just wake up with all this information about a couple of total strangers in my head.

I wasn't going to call again. Once had been bad enough. But twice—well, that was pushing it. I mean, I didn't even know whether or not the information I'd given Rosemary had been accurate. What if it turned out to be totally bogus? What if, by some fluke, that really *hadn't* been Sean Patrick O'Hanahan? What if it had just been some random kid, and I'd totally freaked him out. . . .

No. It *had* been him. I remembered the way he'd gone so pale beneath those freckles. It had been Sean, all right.

And if I'd been right about Sean . . .

The first break I got, I was on the pay phone by the ladies' room, on hold with 1-800-WHERE-R-YOU. I couldn't believe they'd put me on hold. How many people could be calling in on a Saturday afternoon? Jeesh. I only got a five-minute break, and I hadn't even gone to the bathroom yet. The minutes were ticking by, and a family had come in and sat down at one of the tables I hadn't bused yet. They were sitting there, pushing all the empty glasses and used plates into this big, precarious pile. I swear to God, people do not know how to act.

Finally, this woman picked up and asked how she could help me. I went, "Rosemary?"

"No," the woman said. She was white and Southern, I could tell. "Rosemary's not in today. This is Judith. How may I help you?"

I said, "Oh, well, I think I know where these two kids are. Um, Hadley Grant and Timothy Jonas Mills?"

Judith went, "Oh?" in this way suspicious voice.

"Yeah," I said. The family at the table I still hadn't bused was starting to look around in an angry way. One of their kids had tried to drink the leftover ice in one of the used glasses. "Look, Hadley's at—" And I gave her the exact address, which happened to be in Florida. "—and Timothy's in Kansas." I gave her the street address. "Did you get all that?"

"Excuse me, miss," Judith said. "Are you the—"

I said, "Sorry, gotta go," and hung up, mostly because the family was starting to pile the dirty plates on a table that had just opened up beside theirs, but also because I thought Judith had been about to yell at me about Sean and Olivia, and that I did not need.

But after I hung up, I felt better. Just like yesterday. I felt like a weight had been lifted off me.

At least until Pat told me I couldn't bus anymore, and sent me in the back to wash dishes.

The rest of the weekend passed pretty much without incident. On Saturday night, Ruth came over, and this time she actually brought her cello. We played a concerto, then watched some videos she'd rented. Mike came down for a little while and teased us about our taste in movies. Ruth only likes movies that have a beauty makeover in them. Like *Pretty Woman*, when Julia Roberts gets all the clothes. I tend to like movies with explosions. There's only a few movies that have both. *Point of No Return*, with Bridget Fonda, is about the only one. We've seen that movie nine times.

Douglas popped in, too, for a few minutes, on his way to the kitchen to dump off some cereal bowls that had been in his room for a few weeks. He watched the movie for a little while, but then my mom caught him, and started asking if he felt all right. So he had to run back upstairs and hide.

Around eleven o'clock, I could have sworn I heard the purr of Rob Wilkins's Indian outside our house. But when I looked out the window, there was no one there. Wishful thinking, I guess. He was probably totally freaked-out by what an inexperienced kisser I am, and would never ask me out again.

Oh, well. His loss.

Sunday, after church, my dad dumped us off

at Mastriani's to help with the brunch crowd. Well, me and Mike, anyway. Douglas doesn't have to go to church anymore. Instead, he stays home and reads comic books. I know Douglas is sick and all, but I wouldn't mind staying home on Sunday morning and reading comic books. Or watching TV, even. But I never tried to kill myself, so I have to go to church. And I have to go in a dress that matches my mother's.

It's enough to make a girl think there might not actually be a God.

The only thing that happened on Sunday was that we ran out of milk, and my mom sent me and Mike to the store to buy some. Mike let me drive on the way there, but then, on the way back, he totally wouldn't let me near the wheel. But you know, I think speed limits are really just suggestions. If there's nobody else on the road, you should be able to go as fast as you want. Unfortunately, Mike—and your friends at the Department of Motor Vehicles, who keep refusing to give me a license—disagree.

At the grocery store, I picked out a milk carton that had some kids on it I hadn't seen already, just as a kind of experiment. It was slotted to expire in two days, but the way Douglas chows, I knew we'd need more by tomorrow, anyway. Douglas can eat an entire family-size box of Cheerios in one sitting. It's a wonder he isn't fat. But he's always had a very high metabolism, like Mr. Goodhart.

Also at the grocery store, we ran into Claire Lippman. She was standing by the magazine rack, reading *Cosmo,* while her mom was rooting through the corn in the vegetable section. Mike stared at her longingly for a while. Finally I got sick of it, and poked him and said, "Just go *talk* to her, for God's sake."

Mike went, "Oh, right. About what?"

"Tell her you can't wait to see her in *Endgame.*"

"What's that?"

"It's a play. She's in it. She plays Nell. She has to sit in a plastic trash can all during the show."

Mike looked at me. "How do you know? Since when are you in the drama club?"

I realized I had made a mistake. I said, "God, never mind. Come on, let's go."

Only Mike wouldn't go. He just kept staring at Claire. "I mean," he said, "it's not like she'd go with me. If I asked her. Why would she go with me? I don't even have a car."

"You could have bought a car," I said, "with all the money you earned working at the restaurant. But, no. You had to buy that stupid scanner."

"And a printer," Mike said. "And a Zip drive. And—"

"Oh, my God," I said. "Whatever. You can always borrow Dad's car."

"Yeah," Mike said. "A Volvo station wagon. Right. Come on. Let's go."

God. I can't believe boys. It's a wonder anybody gets married at all.

Nothing else much happened on Sunday,
except that that night, while I was practicing, I
thought I heard a motorcycle going down our
street again. And this time, when I looked out my
window, the one I can see the whole street on, I
saw one set of tail lights, way down Lumley
Lane, making the turn off onto Hunter.

Hey, it could have been Rob. You never know.

I went to bed all happy, thinking maybe a boy
liked me. It's stupid that that's all it takes, sometimes, to make you happy. Thinking that someone likes you, I mean. It's especially stupid in
light of what happened the next day. I had way
bigger problems, it turned out, than whether or
not a boy liked me.

Way bigger.

CHAPTER

9

What happened was, the next day, Ruth drove me to school as usual. All during the drive, I couldn't get those kids out of my head. The kids on the side of the milk carton I'd bought the night before, I mean. Once again, I'd wakened with this feeling that I knew exactly where they were, down to the street address. It was getting creepy, let me tell you.

But just like on Friday and Saturday, I couldn't stop thinking about them. So, as soon as we got to school, and I managed to ditch Ruth, I gave old 1-800-WHERE-R-YOU a call. This time Rosemary answered.

"Hey, Rosemary," I said. "It's me, Jess. From Friday, remember?"

Rosemary sucked in her breath. "Jess!" she said. Actually, she practically screamed it in my ear. "Honey, where are you?"

I thought it was kind of funny that somebody who worked for 1-800-WHERE-R-YOU would be asking where *I* was. I went, "Well, right now I'm at school."

"People are looking for you, hon," Rosemary said. "Did you call here on Saturday?"

"Yeah," I said. "Why?"

"Hold on," Rosemary said. "I have to get my supervisor. I promised I would if you called back."

The late bell rang. I went, "Wait, Rosemary. I don't have time. I have to tell you about Jennie Lee Peters and Samantha Travers—"

"Jess," Rosemary said. "Honey, I don't think you understand. Haven't you looked at a newspaper? They found them. They found Sean and Olivia, exactly where you said they'd be. And the children you called about on Saturday—they found them, too. People here want to talk to you, honey. They want to know how you knew—"

So it had been Sean. It had been Sean, after all. Why had he told me his name was Sam? Why had he looked so scared when it was clear I was there to try to help him?

I said, in reply to Rosemary's question, "I don't know how I knew. Look, Rosemary, I'm gonna be late. Just let me tell you—"

"Here's my supervisor, Larry Barnes," Rosemary said. "Larry, it's her. It's Jess."

This man's voice came on over the phone. "Jess?" he said. "Is this Jess?"

"Look," I said. I was getting kind of scared. I mean, I just wanted to help out some missing kids. I didn't want to have to talk to Larry the supervisor. "Jennie Lee Peters is in Escondido, California." I rattled off the address really fast. "And Samantha Travers, it's kind of weird about her, but if you go down Rural Route 4, just outside of Wilmington, Alabama, you'll find her by this tree, this tree with a big rock next to it—"

"Jess," Larry said. "It's Jessica, isn't it? May I have your last name, Jess? And where you're calling from?"

I saw Mrs. Pitt, the Home Ec teacher, waddling toward me. Mrs. Pitt totally hates me because of the time I poured a soufflé over another kid's head in her class, even though he deserved it for asking me how it felt to have a retard for a brother. Mrs. Pitt would not hesitate to write me up.

"Gotta go," I said, and hung up.

But it didn't matter. Mrs. Pitt was like, "Jessica Mastriani, what are you doing out of class?" And then she wrote me up.

Thanks a lot, Mrs. Pitt. I'd like to record my gratitude for your caring and understanding right here in my *statement*, which, I understand, will be made public someday, so that everyone in the whole world will know just how fine a teacher you are.

At lunch, I went to see Mr. Goodhart about

being written up. He said all the usual stuff about how I need to start applying myself more, and how I'm never going to get into college at this rate, etc. After he gave me another week's detention for my own good, I asked him if he had any newspapers, because I had to do a current event for U.S. History.

This was a total lie, of course. I just wanted to see if Rosemary was right.

Mr. Goodhart gave me a copy of *USA Today*. I sat down in the waiting area and looked all through it. There were many entertaining stories about celebrities doing foolish things that distracted me, but finally I found it, this story in the "Nation" section, about an anonymous caller who had contacted 1-800-WHERE-R-YOU and told them the exact location of four children, one of whom had been missing from his home for seven years.

Sean.

I stared at the article. *Me,* I kept thinking. *I* was the anonymous caller. *I* was in the newspaper. A *national* newspaper.

The National Organization for Missing Children wanted to know who I was, so they could extend their thanks.

There was also, it turned out, a substantial reward for finding Olivia Marie D'Amato. Ten thousand bucks, to be exact.

Ten thousand bucks. You could get a heck of a motorcycle for ten thousand bucks.

But then, on the heels of that thought came another: I can't take *money* for doing what I'd done. I mean, I never paid much attention in church, but one thing that had managed to sink in was the fact that you're *supposed* to do nice things for people. You don't do them because you expect to get paid for them. You do it because it's the right thing to do. Like punching Jeff Day, for instance. That had been the right thing to do. Accepting reward money for doing the right thing . . . well, that just seemed wrong to me.

Since I didn't want any lousy reward—and since I didn't want my picture in *USA Today*—I decided not to call NOMC. I mean, it wasn't as if I really wanted anyone to know about this thing I could do. I was enough of a reject at school already. If people found out about this, I'd end up like Carrie, or something, with pig blood all over me. Who needed the hassle?

Besides, the last thing my family could survive was another crisis. My mother hadn't even begun to get over what had happened to Douglas. Although I suspect finding out your kid is psychic is better than finding out he's schizophrenic, it still adds up to one thing: Not Normal. All my mother has ever wanted was to have a normal family.

Though what's so normal about two women wearing the same homemade dress, I cannot begin to imagine.

But still. I did not need the added pressure. I
had enough of my own.

So I didn't call 1-800-WHERE-R-YOU back. I
didn't call anybody. I just went along, doing my
normal thing. At lunch, Ruth teased me about dat-
ing a Grit in front of some of our other friends from
Orchestra, so they started teasing me, too. I didn't
mind, though. I knew they were just jealous. And
they had every right to be. Rob Wilkins was hot.
When I strolled into detention after school that day,
I have to admit, my heart kind of skipped a beat
when I saw him. The guy is good-looking.

We didn't have a chance to speak before Miss
Clemmings cracked the whip. But after she did,
and I took out my notebook and started doing
my homework, Rob didn't lean over and grab it
and start writing cute little notes to me, like he
had on Friday. Instead he just sat there, reading
his spy novel. It was a different spy novel from
the one he'd had last week, and I suppose it was
pretty engrossing and all, but come on. He could
at least have said hi.

The fact that he didn't made me cranky. I suppose other girls would have gotten the message,
but I had no experience in that department. I
couldn't figure out what I had done. Was it the
way I'd reacted when he'd kissed me? You know,
almost falling off the back of his bike like that?
I'll admit, that was pretty juvenile, but give me a
break: it was my first kiss.

Maybe it was the girlfriend-store remark. Or

the fact that I so obviously didn't fit in with Teri and Charleen. The fact that I didn't know made me even more cranky.

Which would probably explain why, when Hank Wendell leaned over and whispered, "Hey, Mastriani, what's this I hear about Wilkins slipping you the sausage last Friday?" I elbowed him in the throat.

Not hard enough to crush his larynx and cause him to lose consciousness (unfortunately), but hard enough to make him really, really mad.

But before Hank's fist could connect with my face (I was fully prepared to roll with the punch, as my father had taught me), this hand shot out, and Hank's arm was twisted up and out of my line of vision.

"I thought we agreed you were going to leave her alone." Rob had to lean over me to keep his grip on Hank. Consequently, his belt buckle was level with my nose. Not exactly a very dignified position.

It made me mad. Almost as mad as Hank's remark.

"Have you been going around telling people we had *sex?*" I demanded, craning my neck to see Rob's face.

Over on the stage, rehearsal had stopped dead. All the cast members of *Endgame* were staring at us. Miss Clemmings was going, "What's happening back there? Mr. Wilkins, release Mr. Wendell and sit down at once!"

"Jesus, Wilkins," Hank said in a strangled voice. Maybe I'd gotten him harder than I thought. "You're breaking my goddamned arm."

"I'll snap it off," Rob said, in this very scary voice I had never heard him use before, "if you don't leave her alone."

"Jesus, all right," Hank said, and Rob let him go.

Hank collapsed back into his seat. Rob retired to his. And Miss Clemmings, who'd been halfway up the aisle, paused and said, "That's better," in this very satisfied voice, as if the fight had broken up on account of something she'd done.

Right.

I was furious.

"What did he mean?" I hissed at Rob as soon as Miss Clemmings's back was turned. "What was he talking about?"

"Nothing," Rob said. He buried his face back in his book. "He's an asshole. Just cool it, will you?"

Okay, I might as well let you know now that one thing I really hate is when people tell me to cool it. For instance, people often make cracks about Douglas, and then tell me to cool it when I get mad. And I can't. I can't cool it.

"No, I will not cool it," I snarled. "I want to know what he was talking about. What the hell is going on? Did you tell your friends we *did it*?"

Rob looked up from his book then. He had

absolutely no expression on his face as he said, "First of all, Wendell is not my friend."

On my left, Hank, still massaging his wrist, grunted. "You got that right."

"Secondly," Rob went on, "I didn't tell anybody anything about you, okay? So just calm down."

I hate it when people tell me to calm down, too.

"Look," I said. "I don't know what's going on here. But if I find out you've been telling people stuff about me behind my back, I will pound you. Understand?"

For the first time all day, he smiled at me. It was like he didn't want to, but he couldn't help it.

And Rob, well, he has one of *those* smiles. You know the kind.

Then again, maybe you don't. I forgot who I was writing this for.

Anyway, he went, *"You're* going to pound *me?"* in this very amused voice. Which just made me madder.

"Don't, man," Hank warned him. "She hits really hard, for a girl."

"Yeah," I said. "So you better watch it."

I don't know what—if anything—Rob would have replied, since Miss Clemmings went "Shhh," just then, in this way I suppose she meant to be threatening. Rob, looking as expressionless as ever, buried his head back in his book.

I had no choice but to turn back to my home-work.

But inside, I was fuming.

I was fuming even harder when, after Miss Clemmings let us go for the day, I walked outside and found that I had no ride home. Like an idiot, I had told Ruth not to bother picking me up. I had assumed Rob would give me a ride home.

Great. Just great.

I could have called my mom, I guess. But I was too wound up to stand around and wait for her. I felt like, if I didn't hit somebody, I would lose it. And when I feel like that, it's better not to be around people. Especially my mom.

So I just started walking. I didn't care about the two miles. I couldn't even feel my feet, I was that mad. It was nice out, not a cloud in the sky. No wor-rying about being struck by lightning today. Not that I cared. A thousand bolts of lightning could come down out of the sky and I wouldn't even notice.

How could I have been so stupid? How could I have been so *dumb*?

I was walking parallel to the bleachers—scene of the crime—when I heard the purr of Rob's bike. He was coasting along by the curb.

"Jess," he said. "Come on."

I didn't even look at him. "Get lost," I said. I really meant it, too.

"What are you going to do, walk all the way home? Come on, I'll give you a ride."

I told him where he could stick his ride.

"Look," he said. "I'm sorry. I made a mistake, all right?"

I thought he was talking about having ignored me in detention.

"You better believe it," I said.

"I just thought you were older, okay?"

That stopped me right in my tracks. I turned around and looked at him.

"What do you mean, you thought I was *older?*" I demanded.

He didn't have his helmet on, so I could see his face. He looked uncomfortable.

"I didn't know you were only sixteen, okay? I mean, you don't act like a sixteen-year-old. You seem a lot more mature. Well, except for the whole punching-guys-who-are-a-lot-bigger-than-you-are thing."

I was having trouble making sense of this.

"What the hell does it matter," I demanded, "how old I am?"

"It matters," he said.

"I don't see why."

"It just does," he said.

I shook my head. "I still don't see why."

"Because I'm eighteen." He wasn't looking at me. He was looking at the road beneath his boots. "And I'm on probation."

Probation? I had been out with a *felon?* My mom was going to die if she ever found out.

"What'd you do?" I asked.

"Nothing."

A Volkswagen went by, honking its horn. Rob was pulled way off to the side of the road, so I couldn't see what the problem was. Then the driver waved. It was Miss Clemmings. Toot-toot. Buh-bye, kids. See you in detention tomorrow.

"No, seriously," I said. "What'd you do?"

"Look," Rob said. "It was stupid, all right?"

"I want to know."

"Well, I'm not going to tell you, so you'd better just forget about it."

My imagination was working overtime. What had he done? Robbed a bank? No, you don't get probation for that. You go to jail. Ditto if he'd killed someone. What could he have done?

"So, I don't think it's such a good idea," he went on. "Us going out, I mean. Unless . . . When's your birthday?"

"Just had it last month," I said.

He said a word that I will refrain from recording here.

"Look," I said. "I don't care that you're on probation."

"Yeah, but your parents will."

"No, they're cool."

He laughed. "Right, Jess. That's why you made me drop you off at the end of the street the other night, instead of in front of your house. Because your parents are so cool. They're so cool, you didn't want them to know anything about

me. And you didn't even know about the probation thing then. Admit it."

He had me there.

"Well," I said. "They're just going through sort
of a hard time right now, and I don't want to
cause them any more stress. But look, there's no
reason they have to know."

"Word gets around, Jess. Look at Wendell.
It's only a matter of time before your parents—
and my probation officer—get wind of what's
going on."

Well, I wasn't going to stand there and beg
him to go out with me. The guy was hot and
everything, but a girl has her pride. So I just
shrugged and said, "Whatever."

Then I turned around and started walking
again.

"Mastriani," he said, in a tired voice. "Look,
just get on the bike, will ya? I'll take you home.
Or to your street corner, I guess."

"I don't know," I said, looking back at him
and fluttering my eyelashes. "I mean, Miss
Clemmings already saw us together. Supposing
she goes running to the cops—"

He looked annoyed. "Just get on the bike,
Mastriani."

I can tell what you're thinking.

You're thinking that, in spite of the whole
jailbait thing, Rob and I went on to have this
totally hot and steamy relationship, and that I'm
going to go into all the lurid details right here in

my *statement*, and that you're going to get to read all about it.

Well, sorry to disappoint you, but that is so not going to happen. In the first place, my love life is my own business, and the only reason I mention it here is that it becomes pertinent later on.

And in the second place, Rob didn't lay a finger on me.

Much to my chagrin.

No, he dropped me off, as promised, on the corner, and I walked the rest of the way home, cursing the fact that I have to live in this backward state with its backward laws. I mean, a sixteen-year-old girl can't date an eighteen-year-old boy in the state of Indiana, but it's perfectly okay for first cousins to marry at any age.

I'm serious. Look it up if you don't believe me.

As usual when I got home that night, there was a commotion going on in the kitchen. This one involved my mom and dad and Douglas (big surprise). Douglas was standing there, looking down at the floor, while my mom yelled at my dad.

"I told you he wasn't ready!" she was screaming. My mom has a pretty healthy set of lungs on her. "I told you! But did you listen? Oh, no. Big Joe Mastriani always knows what's best."

"The kid did great," my dad said. "Really great. Okay, so he dropped a tray and broke some stuff. Big deal. Trays get dropped every day. It doesn't mean—"

"He's not ready," my mom yelled.

Douglas saw me in the doorway. I rolled my eyes at him. He just looked back down at the floor again. There are kids, back at school, who say things to me about my "psycho" brother, about how he's been voted most likely to be a serial killer, and that kind of thing. That's one of the reasons I have detention from now until the foreseeable future. Because I've had to slug so many people for talking dirt about Douglas. But I don't think Douglas could ever be a serial killer. He's way too shy. That Ted Bundy guy, he was pretty outgoing, from what I heard.

My dad noticed me in the doorway and went, "Where have you been?" only not in a mean way.

"Band practice," I said.

"Oh," my dad said. Then he started yelling at my mom some more.

I grabbed a bowl of cereal—checking the milk carton, of course. As I'd suspected, my mom had seen the expired date and run out to buy a new one. I studied the faces of the kids on this particular box. I wondered if, in the morning, I would know where they lived. I had a feeling I would. After all, the mark on my chest, where the lightning had struck me, was still there. It hadn't faded hardly at all.

I wondered how Sean was doing. By now he'd probably been joyfully reunited with his family. He owed me, I thought, one heck of a big thank you. And an apology for acting like such a little headcase that day outside his house.

I went upstairs, but before I got to my room, Mike scared the bejesus out of me by tearing open, not his bedroom door, but Douglas's, and going, "All right. Who the hell is he?"

I had slammed back against the hallway wall in my surprise at seeing him come out of nowhere like that. I went, "Who the hell is who? And what were you doing in Douglas's room?"

Then I saw the binoculars in his hand, and I knew.

"Okay," I said. "It's not what you think."

"Oh, yeah?" Mike glared at me through the lenses of his glasses. "What I think is that you are slutting around with some Hell's Angel. That's what I think."

"You are so lame," I said. "He isn't a Hell's Angel, and I am not slutting around with anybody."

"Then who is he?"

"God, he's in your class, all right? He's a senior. His name is Rob Wilkins."

"Rob Wilkins?" Mike glared down at me some more. "I don't know any senior named Rob Wilkins."

"Color me surprised," I said. "You don't know anyone whose name isn't followed by an *A* in a little circle and the words *AOL dot com.*"

He wasn't letting me off the hook though, no matter how hard I dissed him.

"What is he?" Mike demanded. "A dropout?"

"No," I said. "Not that it's any business of yours."

"Well, then, how come I don't know him?" Then Mike's jaw dropped. "Oh, my God. Is he a *Grit*?"

"Gosh, Mike," I said. "That is so PC of you. I bet your new friends at Harvard are just going to love your open-minded attitude."

Mike shook his head. "Mom is going to *kill* you."

"No, she isn't, because you aren't going to tell her."

"Like fun I'm not," Mike declared. "I don't want my little sister going out with a Grit."

"We aren't going out," I said. "And if you don't tell Mom, I'll . . . I'll take your shift at the restaurant this weekend."

He brightened up, his protectiveness for his little sister forgotten. Hey, why not? More time on the Internet for him.

"Really?" he asked. "The Sunday night one, too?"

I sighed, like this was a big sacrifice, when really, I would have worked *all* his shifts for the rest of my natural life if he'd asked me to, in order to keep Mom from finding out about Rob.

"Sunday night, too, I guess," I said.

Mike looked triumphant. Then he seemed to remember he was my older brother, and he was supposed to look out for me and stuff, because he said, "Don't you think a senior is a little old for you? I mean, after all, you're just a sopho-more."

I said, "Don't worry, Mikey. I can handle myself."

He still looked worried, though. "I know, but what if this guy . . . you know. Tries something?"

It was my fondest wish that he would. Unfortunately, it did not look like this was going to happen.

"Look," I said. "Don't worry about it. Seriously, Mike. You just keep on spying on Claire Lippman, and let me do the actual making out, okay?"

Mike turned kind of red, but I didn't feel sorry for him. He was blackmailing me, after all.

That night, after I'd gone to bed, my mind was too filled with the whole Rob problem to think about what was going on, you know, with the psychic thing. I mean, the missing-kid stuff just didn't seem that important.

Of course, that changed completely, the next day.

CHAPTER

10

Rosemary sounded strange when I called her the next morning. Maybe it was because someone else had answered at first, and I had been all, "Is Rosemary there?" The man who had answered had said, "One moment, please," and then I'd heard a click, and then Rosemary came on.

"Hey," I said. "It's me, Jess."

"Hi, Jess," she said. But she didn't sound as excited as she had the day before. "How are you doing, honey?"

I said, "Fine. I got some more addresses for you."

She didn't sound like she was any too eager to take them down, though. She said, "I don't suppose you saw the paper, did you, hon?"

"About the reward, you mean?" I scraped at

the words *Fuck You*, which someone had carved into the metal door over the change slot of the pay phone I was using. "Yeah, I saw about the reward. But that seems kind of wrong to me. Collecting a reward, for something any decent human being would do for free. Know what I mean?"

Rosemary said, "Oh, I know what you mean, honey. But that isn't what I was talking about. I was talking about the little girl you called about yesterday. You told Larry they'd find her by a tree."

"Oh," I said. I was keeping an eagle eye out for Mrs. Pitt. I was determined not to let her catch me this time. All I saw, however, was a black car that had pulled up in the teachers' parking lot. Two men in suits got out of it. Undercover cops, I thought. Somebody had obviously narked on somebody. "Yeah. I thought that was kind of strange. What was she doing by that tree, any-way?"

Rosemary said, "She wasn't by the tree, honey. She was under it. She was dead. Somebody mur-dered her and buried the body where you said they'd find it." Then Rosemary said, "Honey? Jess? Are you still there?"

I went, "Yeah. Yeah, I'm here." Dead? Little Whatever-Her-Name-Had-Been? Dead?

This wasn't so fun anymore.

And then it *really* wasn't fun. Because I noticed that the two undercover cops were walking toward *me*. I thought they'd been going into the administrative offices, which would have made sense, but instead, they walked right up to *me*.

Up close, I could see that they both had very short hair, and that they were both wearing suits. One of them reached into his breast pocket. When his hand came out again, it was holding a small wallet, which he flipped open and held out toward me.

"Hello, there," he said in a pleasant voice. "I'm Special Agent Chet Davies, and this is my partner, Special Agent Allan Johnson. We're with the FBI. We have some questions we'd like to ask you, Jess. Will you hang up the phone and come with us, please?"

In my ear, I could hear Rosemary saying, "Jess, honey, I'm so sorry, I didn't want to have anything to do with it, but they made me."

Special Agent Chet Davies took me by the arm. He said, "Come on, sweetheart. Hang up the phone."

I don't know what made me do it. To this day, I don't know what made me do it. But instead of hanging up the phone, like the agent asked, I punched him in the face with the receiver as hard as I could.

And then I ran.

I didn't go very far, though. I mean, once I started running, I realized how stupid I was being. Where was I going to go? I had no car. How far was I going to get on foot? This was the

FBI. It wasn't our Podunk town cops, who are so fat they couldn't chase a cow, let alone a sixteen-year-old girl who'd won the two-hundred-yard dash in P.E. every year since she was ten.

No offense, guys.

But it was like I went mental or something. And when I go mental, I usually end up in the same place. So I decided to cut to the chase and go where I'd probably end up anyway. I ran into the counseling office, threw open Mr. Goodhart's door, and collapsed into the orange vinyl chair by the window.

Mr. Goodhart was eating a cheese Danish. He looked at me over it and said, "Why, Jess, what a pleasant surprise. What brings you here so bright and early?"

I was panting a little. I said, "Two FBI guys just tried to pull me into their car for questioning, but I punched one of them in the face and came here instead."

Mr. Goodhart picked up a coffee mug that had Snoopy on it and took a sip from it. Then he said, "Okay, Jess, let's try that again. I say, 'What brings you here so bright and early,' and you say something like, 'Oh, I don't know, Mr. Goodhart. I just thought I'd drop in to talk about the fact that I'm doing poorly in English again, and I was wondering if you could help convince Miss Kovax to give me some extra credit.' "

Then Mr. Goodhart's secretary, Helen,

appeared in the doorway. She looked flustered. "Paul," she said. "There're two men here—"

But she didn't get to finish, because Special Agent Chet Davies pushed her out of the way. He was holding a handkerchief to his nose, from which blood was streaming. He waved his badge at Mr. Goodhart, but his gaze, which was blazing, was on me.

"That was pretty slick," he said, sounding a bit nasal, which wasn't surprising, since I guess I'd broken some cartilage or something. "But assaulting a federal agent happens to be a felony, little lady. Get up. We're going for a drive."

I didn't get up. But just as Special Agent Davies was reaching for me, Mr. Goodhart went, "Excuse me."

That's all. Just, "Excuse me."

But Special Agent Davies pulled his hand away from me as if I'd been on fire or something. Then he threw Mr. Goodhart this very guilty look.

"Oh," he said. He groped for his badge. "Special Agent Chet Davies. I'm taking this girl in for questioning."

Mr. Goodhart actually picked up his Danish, took a bite, and put it down again before he said, "Not without her parents, you're not. She's a minor."

Special Agent Allan Johnson showed up then. He flashed his badge, introduced himself, and said, "Sir, I don't know if you're aware of the fact that this young lady is wanted for questioning in several kidnapping cases, as well as a murder."

Mr. Goodhart looked at me with his eyebrows raised.

"You've been busy, haven't you, Jess?"

I said, in a croaky voice, because suddenly I was as close to crying as I'd ever been, "I was just talking on the phone, and then these two men I've never seen before told me I had to get into a car with them. Well, my mother told me never to get into cars with strangers, and even though they said they were FBI agents and they had those badges and all, how was I supposed to know they were real? I've never seen an FBI badge before. And that's why I hit him, and, Mr. Goodhart—I'm afraid I'm going to cry."

Mr. Goodhart said, in his teasing way, "You aren't going to cry, Jess. You weren't really afraid of these two clowns, were you?"

"Yes," I said with a sob. "I really was. Mr. Goodhart, I don't want to go to jail!"

By the end of all that, I'm embarrassed to say I wasn't close to crying anymore. I *was* crying. I was practically bawling.

But, come on. You would have been scared, too, if the FBI wanted to question you.

While I was sniffling and wiping my eyes and blaming Ruth in my head for this whole mess, Mr. Goodhart looked at the FBI guys and said, in a voice that wasn't teasing at all, "You two go and have a seat in the outer office. She isn't going

anywhere until her parents—and their lawyer—
get here."

You could tell by Mr. Goodhart's face that he
meant it, too. I had never felt such a wave of
affection for him as I did at that moment. I mean,
he may have doled out the detentions pretty
strictly, but he was a stand-up kind of guy when
you needed him.

The two FBI guys seemed to realize this.
Special Agent Davies swore loudly. His partner
looked a little embarrassed for him. He said to
me, "Look, we didn't mean to scare you, Miss.
We just wanted to ask you a few questions, that's
all. Maybe we could find someplace quiet where
we could just straighten out this mess."

"Sure you can," Mr. Goodhart said. "After her
parents get here."

Special Agent Johnson knew when he'd been
beat. He nodded and went into the outer office,
sat down, and picked up a copy of *Seventeen* and
started to flip through it. Special Agent Davies,
on the other hand, said another swear word and
began pacing up and down in the outer office,
while Helen, the secretary, watched him ner-
vously.

Mr. Goodhart didn't look nervous at all. He
took another sip of coffee, then picked up the
phone. "Okay, Jess," he said. "Who's it going to
be—your mother, or your father?"

I was still crying pretty hard. I said, "M-my
dad. Oh, please, my dad."

Mr. Goodhart called my dad at Mastriani's, where he was working that morning. Since neither of my parents had ever been called to school on account of me—in spite of all the fights I'd been in—I could hear urgency in my dad's voice as he asked Mr. Goodhart if I was all right. Mr. Goodhart assured him that I was, but that he might want to call his lawyer, if he had one. My dad, God bless him, hung up with a brisk, "We'll be there in five minutes." He never once even asked why.

After Mr. Goodhart hung up, he looked over at me, then reached for some tissues he kept in a box for the losers who sat in his office and cried all day about their unsatisfactory family life, or whatever.

I'm one of those losers now, I thought, as I dejectedly blew my nose.

"Tell me about it," Mr. Goodhart said.

And so, with a nervous glance at the FBI guys, to make sure they couldn't overhear, I did. I told Mr. Goodhart everything, from getting hit by the lightning all the way up until that morning, when Special Agent Davies flashed his badge. The only stuff I left out was the parts about Rob. I didn't figure Mr. Goodhart needed to know that.

By the time I got done telling Mr. Goodhart, my dad had arrived with our lawyer, who also happened to be Ruth's dad, Mr. Abramowitz. Special Agent Davies had recovered himself by then, and he acted like nothing had happened.

Like he hadn't tried to grab me, and like I hadn't hit him in the face with a phone receiver.

Oh, no. Nothing of the sort. He was way professional as he told my dad and Mr. Abramowitz about how the FBI was very interested in the person who'd been making calls to the National Organization of Missing Children from the pay phone at which they'd found me. Apparently, at 1-800-WHERE-R-YOU, they had caller-ID phones, so Rosemary had known from the very first day I'd been calling from Indiana. All they needed to do was track down where in Indiana, then actually catch me making the call.

Then, *voilà*, as my mom would say, they had me.

Of course, the big question was what, now that they had me, were they going to do with me? As far as I knew, I hadn't actually broken any laws—well, except for striking a federal agent, and Special Agent Davies didn't seem all that anxious to bring that up again.

All the excitement—having two FBI agents, a father, and a lawyer in his counseling offices— had dragged out the principal, Mr. Feeney. Mr. Feeney rarely came out of his office, except sometimes during assembly to remind us not to drink and drive. Now he offered us the use of his private conference room, where we sat, the seven of us—me, my dad, Ruth's dad, the two special agents, Mr. Goodhart, and Mr. Feeney—while I repeated the story I'd just told Mr. Goodhart.

I guess you could say that, when I finished, they looked . . . well, skeptical. And it was kind of hard to believe. I mean, how had it happened? How was it that I just woke up every morning, knowing this totally random stuff about these kids? Yeah, the lightning had probably done it . . . but how? And why?

Nobody knew. My guess was, nobody would ever know.

But Special Agent Johnson, it turned out, really wanted to. Know, I mean. He asked me a ton of questions. Some of them were really weird, too. Like, had I experienced bleeding from my palms or my feet. I said, "Uh, no," and looked at him like he was crazy.

"If this is true," he began, after I thought he'd exhausted all the questions anyone could possibly ask somebody.

"*If* this is true?" my dad interrupted. My dad's not the world's most even-tempered guy. Not that he gets mad a lot. He hardly ever gets mad. But when he does, watch out. One time, this guy at the municipal swimming pool was following Douglas around, calling him a retard—this was when Douglas was like eleven or twelve years old. The guy was in his twenties, at least, and probably not too swift upstairs himself. But that didn't matter to my dad. He hauled off and slugged the guy, and *then* he held his face underwater for a while, until the lifeguard made him stop.

It was way cool.

"*If?*" my dad repeated. "Are you doubting the word of my little girl here?"

Special Agent Johnson probably hadn't heard the story of the guy at the swimming pool, but he looked scared, just the same. Because you could tell my dad was really proud of me. Not just because I hadn't cried this time while I was telling my side of things, but because, when you think about it, what I had done was pretty nifty. I had found a bunch of missing kids. Granted, one of them had been dead, but, hey, we'd never have known that if it hadn't been for me. And considering that he had one kid who was a schizo, and another who was basically a social leper, even if he had gotten into Harvard, well, I guess my dad was kind of stoked that at least one of his kids was making good, you know?

Special Agent Johnson held up a hand and said, "No, sir. Don't misunderstand me. I believe Miss Mastriani's story wholeheartedly. I'm only saying that, if it's true, well, then she's a very special young lady, and deserves some very special treatment."

I thought he might be talking about a ticker-tape parade in New York City, like the one they had for the Yankees that time they won the World Series. I wouldn't mind riding on a float, if it didn't go too slow.

But my dad right away suspected he was talking about something else.

"Like what kind of treatment?" he said, suspiciously.

"Well, usually, in cases like these—and I will have you know that we at the FBI respect those with extrasensory perception like Miss Mastriani's very highly. In fact, we often seek out advice from psychics when we find ourselves at a dead end in an investigation."

"I bet. What does that have to do with Jess?" My dad still sounded suspicious.

"Well, we'd like to invite Miss Mastriani— with your permission, of course, sir—to one of our research facilities, so that we can learn more about this astonishing ability of hers."

I immediately flashed back on one of my favorite videos when I'd been a kid, *Escape to Witch Mountain.* If you've seen that movie, you will recall that the kids in it, who have ESP—or extrasensory perception, as Special Agent Johnson called it—get sent to a special "research facility," where, even though they get their own soda fountain in their room—by which I'd been particularly impressed, since my mother wouldn't even let me have an E-Z Bake Oven for fear I'd burn down the house—they were still, basically, held prisoner.

"Um," I said loudly. Since no one had really been talking to me, everyone turned their heads to look at me. "No, thank you."

Mr. Goodhart, who obviously hadn't seen *Escape to Witch Mountain,* said, "Now, hold on a second, Jess. Let's hear Special Agent Johnson out. It isn't every day that someone with your special ability comes along. It's important that we try to learn as much as possible about what's happened to you, so that we can better under-stand the extraordinary ways in which the human mind works."

I glared at Mr. Goodhart. What a traitor! I couldn't believe it.

"I am not," I said, in a voice that was still too loud for Mr. Feeney's conference room, "going to any special research facility in Washington, D.C."

Special Agent Johnson said, "Oh, but this one is right here in Indiana. Only an hour away, at Crane Military Base, as a matter of fact. There we can adequately study Miss Mastriani's extraordi-nary talent. Maybe she could even help us find more missing people. When you were calling the Missing Children's Organization this morning, Miss Mastriani, it was because you had the loca-tion of yet another missing child, was it not?"

I scowled at him. "Yes," I said. "Not like I ever got the chance to tell them that, though. You two guys made me completely forget the addresses."

This was a complete and utter lie, but I was feeling grumpy. I didn't want to go to Crane Military Base. I didn't want to go anywhere. I wanted to stay where I was. I wanted to go to detention after school today and sit by Rob. When else was I ever going to get to see him?

And what about Karen Sue Hanky? She had

challenged me again. I had to kick her butt one
more time. I *needed* to kick her butt one more
time. *That* was my special ability. Not this freaky
thing that had been happening lately. . . .

"There are many, many more people missing
in the world, Miss Mastriani," Special Agent
Johnson said, "than are pictured on the back of
milk cartons. With your help, we could find missing prisoners of war, for whose safe return their
families have been praying for twenty, even
thirty years. We could locate deadbeat dads, and
make them pay back the money their children so
badly need. We could track down vicious serial
killers, catch them before they can kill again. The
FBI does offer significant cash rewards for information leading to the arrest of individuals for
whom it has issued warrants of arrest."

I could tell my dad was totally falling for this.
I even caught myself falling for it, a little. I mean,
it would be totally cool to reunite families with
their missing loved ones, or to catch bad guys,
and see that they got what they deserved.

But why did I have to go and do it from an
army base?

So I asked him that. And I added, "I mean, it
might not even work. What if I can only find
these people from my own bed, in my own
house? Why would I have to do it from Crane
Military Base? Why couldn't you just let me do it
from Lumley Lane?"

Special Agent Johnson and Special Agent

Davies looked at one another. Everyone else looked at them, too, with *Yeah, why couldn't she?* expressions on their faces.

Finally, Special Agent Johnson said, "Well, you could, Jessica." I noticed he wasn't calling me Miss Mastriani anymore. "Of course you could. But our researchers would dearly love to run some tests. And the fact that all of this seems to have stemmed from being struck by lightning— well, I don't want to sound like an alarmist, but I would think you would welcome those tests. Because we have found in the past that, in cases like yours, there has sometimes been damage to vital internal organs that goes undetected for months, and then . . ."

My dad leaned forward. "And then what?"

"Well, often the individual simply drops dead, Mr. Mastriani, from a heart attack—being struck by lightning puts an incredible strain on the heart. Or of an embolism, aneurism—any number of complications can and often do arise. A thorough medical exam—"

"Which I could have right here," I said, not liking the sound of this. "In Dr. Hinkle's office." Dr. Hinkle had been our family doctor my whole life. He had, of course, misdiagnosed Douglas's schizophrenia as ADD, but hey, we can't all be perfect.

"Certainly," Special Agent Johnson said. "Certainly. Although the general practitioner is not often trained to detect the subtle changes that occur in a system that has been violated in the manner yours has."

"About these cash rewards," Mr. Feeney said suddenly.

I glared at him. What an asshole. I could tell he was totally trying to think up some angle whereby he could get his hands on the reward money, and design a new trophy cabinet for the main hallway, so he could display all of our stupid state championship cups, or whatever. God, I hated school.

That was it. I had had enough. I stood up, pushing back my chair—which was way nicer than any chair in any of the classrooms: it had wheels on it, and was made of some plush, squishy material that surely couldn't have been real leather, or Mr. Feeney would have gotten in trouble with the school board for overspending—and said, "Well, okay, if you're not going to arrest me, I think I'd like to go home now."

Special Agent Johnson said, "We're not through here, Jess."

Then an extraordinary thing happened. My lower lip started to jut out a little—I think I was still feeling a little emotional from that whole they're-gonna-arrest-me scare—and my dad, who noticed, stood up and said, "No."

No. Just like that. No.

"You've intimidated my daughter enough for one day. I'm taking her home to her mother."

Special Agents Johnson and Davies exchanged

glances. They did not want to let me go. But my dad was already walking over to me, picking up my backpack and flute, and laying a hand on my shoulder.

"Come on, Jess," he said. "We're going."

Ruth's dad, meanwhile, was reaching into his pocket. He took out some business cards and dropped them on Mr. Feeney's conference table.

"If you gentlemen need to contact the Mastrianis," he said to the agents, "you can do so through my offices. Have a nice day."

Special Agent Johnson looked disappointed, but all he said was that I should call him the minute I changed my mind about Crane Military Base. Then he gave me his card. Special Agent Davies, as he was leaving the conference room, made a gun out of his index finger and thumb and shot me. I thought this was a little alarming, considering the fact that his nostrils were all crusted over with blood, and a purply bruise was starting to show across the bridge of his nose. . . .

Mr. Feeney was pretty nice about giving me the rest of the day off from class. He never even mentioned a thing about me making up detention, and then I realized that was because he didn't even know I had detention from now until the end of school in May. Mr. Feeney doesn't pay a whole lot of attention to the students.

But Mr. Goodhart, who does, didn't mention making up the detention day either. That's because I had begged him a long time ago not to

pester my parents about anything, what with
Douglas and all. He stuck to his word, though he
did say he wished I would rethink the Crane
Military Base thing. I said I would, even though I
hadn't the slightest intention of doing so.

My dad drove me home. On the way home,
we stopped at a Wendy's, and he bought me a
Frosty. This was sort of a joke, because he used
to buy me a Frosty every day on our way home
from the county hospital, back when I'd had
out-patient treatments for a third-degree burn
I'd gotten on my calf from the exhaust pipe of
our neighbor's Harley. Dr. Feingold, the neurol-
ogist, had bought a completely cherried-out
mint-green Harley-Davidson for his fiftieth
birthday, and when I was a little kid, I used to
beg him for rides, and he'd take me, more often
than not, probably just to shut me up. He
warned me about the exhaust pipe a million
times, but I forgot one day, and wham! Third-
degree burn the size of a fist. I still had the scar,
though the burn ward had worked diligently,
every day for three months, to remove all the
infected skin.

The way they removed it was worse than the
burn itself, though. With tweezers. I used to pass
out every time. Then, to cheer me up, my dad
would take me to Wendy's for a Frosty. So, you
can see that this gesture of his was deeply moving, even though it may not sound like much to
you guys. It was all about sharing this bonding

moment from our past. Mr. Goodhart would have eaten it up.

Anyway, on the way home, my dad agreed to break the news to Mom, but not tell anybody else—I made him swear—and I agreed not to keep any more secrets from him. I still didn't tell him about Rob, though, because that was a secret I strongly suspected the FBI didn't have a lead on, so I probably wasn't going to almost get arrested for it.

Plus I was way more worried about my mom's reaction to finding out about Rob than the story of me and the milk-carton kids.

CHAPTER

11

In the end, of course, it turned out that my dad wasn't the one I ought to have sworn to secrecy.

It was Mr. Feeney.

I don't know if he thought he could get his hands on that reward money somehow, or if he'd decided that spilling the beans would make his school district stand out from all the others in Indiana—like, since it was his school's bleachers I'd gotten electrocuted under, that somehow made Ernest Pyle High School special—or what.

But anyway, when the town paper hit our front porch that afternoon—the town paper came out at three in the afternoon every day, instead of seven in the morning, so the reporters and everybody don't have to get up too early—there was this giant picture of me on the front of it: my very flattering sophomore yearbook picture, in fact, the one in which my mom had made me wear one of her hideous homemade dresses, under a headline that read, TOUCHED BY THE FINGER OF GOD.

Have I pointed out that there are more churches in our town than there are fast-food restaurants? Southern Indiana is way religious.

Anyway, the article went on to describe how I had saved all these kids after being touched by the finger of God, or lightning, as it is called by the secular community. It went on to say that I was just an average student who played third-chair flute in the school orchestra, and that on weekends I helped my dad out in his restaurants, which they listed. I knew all this stuff couldn't have come from Mr. Feeney, since he didn't know me all that well. I figured Mr. Goodhart must have had something to do with it.

And let me tell you, that kind of hurt, you know? I mean, even though he hadn't mentioned anything about the trouble with Douglas, or my detentions, he sure had mentioned everything else he knew. Isn't there some sort of confidentiality thing with school counselors? I mean, can't they get in trouble for that?

But when my dad called Mr. Abramowitz and asked him, he was like, "You can't prove the information came from the counselor. It came from someone at the school, most definitely. But you can't prove it was the counselor."

Still, Ruth's dad started putting together a

lawsuit, aimed at hitting Ernest Pyle High School for slipping the town paper my school photo. That, Mr. Abramowitz said, was an invasion of privacy. He sounded really happy about it. Ruth's dad doesn't get that many interesting cases. Mostly, he just does divorces.

My mother was happy about it, too. Don't ask me why, but the whole story totally delighted her. She was in hog heaven. She wanted me to have a press conference in the main dining room at Mastriani's. She kept going on about how much money it would bring in to the restaurant, feeding all those out-of-town reporters. She even started picking out dress patterns, right then and there, for what she wanted me to wear at this press conference. I'm telling you, she went mental. I had kind of thought she'd be all weird about it, you know? I mean, considering her *I just want us to be a normal family* mentality. But that went right out the window when she heard about the rewards.

"How much?" she wanted to know. "How much per child?"

We were eating dinner at that point—fettucine with a mushroom cream sauce. My dad went, "Toni, the rewards are not the point. The point is, Jessica is a young girl, and I do not want her exposed to the media at such a young—"

"But is it ten thousand dollars per child?" my mother wanted to know. "Or just for that one child?"

"Toni—"

"Joe, I'm just saying, ten thousand dollars is nothing to sneeze at. It could buy a new steam table and then some over at Joe Junior's—"

"We will raise the money for a new steam table over at Joe Junior's the old-fashioned way," my father said. "We will take out a loan for it."

"Not when we're already going to have to take out a loan for Michael's tuition." Michael—whose sole reaction to the news about my new-found psychic ability had been to ask me if I knew where the man in the blue turban, whom Nostradamus had predicted would start World War III, was hanging out these days—rolled his eyes.

"Don't you roll your eyes at me, young man," my mother said. "Harvard was very generous with the scholarship money, but it's still not enough—"

"Especially not," my dad said, dipping his semolina into the cream sauce left on his plate, "if Dougie's going back to State."

That did it. My mom dropped her fork with a clatter. "Douglas," she said, "is not going back to that school. Not ever."

My dad looked tired. "Toni," he said. "The boy's going to have to get an education. He can't sit in that room up there and read comic books for the rest of his life. People are already starting to call him Boo Radley."

Boo Radley, I remembered from freshman

English, was the guy in *To Kill a Mockingbird* who never left his house, just sat around cutting up newspapers all day, which is what people did before there was TV. It was a good thing Douglas had refused to come downstairs for dinner, or he might have heard that and been offended. For a guy who tried to kill himself, Douglas is very sensitive about being called strange.

"Why not?" my mother demanded. "Why can't he sit in his room for the rest of his life? If that's what he wants to do, why can't you just let him?"

"Because nobody gets to do what they want to do, Toni. I want to lie in the backyard in a hammock all day," my dad said, jerking a thumb at his chest. "Jess over there wants to cruise the countryside on the back of a hog. And Mikey—" He looked at Michael, who was busy chewing. "Well, I don't know what the hell Mikey wants to do—"

"Screw Claire Lippman," I suggested, causing Michael to kick me very hard beneath the table.

My dad shot me a warning look, and continued. "But whatever it is, Toni, he doesn't get to do it. Nobody gets to do what they want to do, Toni. What they get to do is what they *should* do, and what Dougie *should* do is go back to college."

Relieved to have some of the heat off me, I excused myself and cleared my place at the table. I hadn't talked to Ruth all day. I was eager to see what she thought of this whole thing. I mean, it isn't every day your best friend ends up on the front page of the local rag.

But I never got to find out what Ruth thought of the whole thing. Because when I stepped outside onto the porch, preparing to jump over the hedge that separated our two houses, I was confronted by what looked like an army of reporters, all of them parked in front of our house and waving cameras and microphones.

"There she is!" One of them, a newscaster I recognized from Channel Four, came stumbling across my lawn, her high heels sinking into the grass. "Jessica! Jessica! How does it feel to be a national heroine?"

I stared down at the fuzzy microphone blankly. Then about a million other microphones appeared in my face. Everyone started asking questions at once. It was my mother's press conference, only all I had on was jeans and a T-shirt. I hadn't even thought to comb my hair.

"Um," I said into the microphones.

Then my dad was there, yanking me back into the house, and yelling at all the reporters to get off his property. No one listened—at least, not until the cops came. Then we got to see how all those free lunches my dad had given the guys on the force paid off. You never saw people as mad as those cops were when they turned down Lumley Lane and couldn't even find a place to park, there were so many news vans blocking the way. There are so few crimes in our neck of the woods that when one did happen, our boys in blue go to town on the offender.

When they saw all the reporters on our lawn, they went mental, only in a different way than my mom had. They called back to the station, and, next thing you knew, they had brought out all their fanciest equipment, riot gear and drug-sniffing dogs and flash grenades. You name it, they brought it over, and looked pretty intent on using it on the reporters, some of whom were from pretty big networks.

I have to say, I was way impressed. Mike and I watched the whole thing from my dormer window. Mike even went on the Internet and ran a search for my name, and said there were already two hundred and seventy sites that mentioned Jessica Mastriani. Nobody had taken my face and superimposed it over a Playboy bunny's naked body, but Mike said it was only a matter of time.

Then the phone started ringing.

The first few calls were from reporters standing outside, using their cell phones. They wanted me to come out and make a statement, just one. Then they promised to leave. My dad hung up on them.

Then people who weren't reporters, but whom we still didn't know, started calling, asking if I was available to help them find a missing relative, a child, a husband, a father. At first my dad was nice to them, and told them that it didn't work that way, that I had to see a picture of the missing person. Then they started saying they'd fax a picture, or e-mail it. Some of them said they were coming right on over with one, they'd be there in a few hours.

That's when my dad disconnected the phone.

I was a celebrity. Or a prisoner in my own house. Whichever you prefer.

I still hadn't gotten to talk to Ruth, and I really wanted to. But since I couldn't go outside or call her, my only resource was to instant-message her from Michael's computer. He was feeling sorry for me, so, in spite of my crack about Claire Lippman, he let me.

Ruth, however, wasn't too pleased to hear from me.

Ruth: Why the HELL didn't you tell me about any of this?

Me: Look, Ruth, I didn't tell *anybody*, okay? It was all just too weird.

Ruth: But I'm supposed to be your best friend.

Me: You *are* my best friend.

Ruth: Well, I bet you told Rob Wilkins.

Me: I swear I didn't.

Ruth: Oh, right. You don't tell the guy you're boffing that you're psychic. I really believe that one.

Me: First of all, I am not boffing Rob Wilkins. Second of all, do you really think I wanted anyone to know about this? It's totally freaky. You know I like to keep a low profile.

Ruth: It was totally uncool of you not to tell me. Do you
    know people from school have been calling, asking
    me if I knew, and I've had to pretend like I did, just
    to save face? You are the worst best friend I've ever
    had.

Me: I'm the *only* best friend you've ever had. And you
    don't have any right to be mad, since it's all your
    fault anyway, for making me walk in that stupid
    thunderstorm.

Ruth: What are you going to do with the reward
    money? You know, I could really use a new stereo
    for the Cabriolet. And Skip says to tell you he wants
    the new Tomb Raider.

Me: Tell Skip I said I'm not buying him anything until
    he apologizes for that whole strapping-my-Barbie-
    to-the-bottle-rocket business.

Ruth: You know, I don't see how any of us are going to
    be able to get to school tomorrow. The street is
    totally blocked. It looks like a scene out of *Red
    Dawn* down there.

The truth was, Ruth was right. With the cops
forming this protective shield in front of my
house, and our driveway all blockaded, it sort of
did look like the Russians were coming or something. No one could get up or down our street
without flashing an ID that proved they lived
there to the cops. For instance, if Rob wanted to
cruise by on his Indian—not that he would want
to, but let's say he took a wrong turn, or what-

ever—he totally couldn't. The cops wouldn't let him through.

I tried not to let this bother me. I logged off with Ruth, after assuring her that, though I hadn't told her, I hadn't told anyone else, either, which seemed to placate her somewhat, especially after I told her, if she wanted to, she could tell everyone she'd already known—I certainly didn't care. This made her very happy, and I suppose after she logged off with me, she logged on with Muffy and Buffy and all of the pathetic popular kids whose friendship she so assiduously courts, for reasons I had never been able to fathom.

I took out my flute and practiced for a while, but to tell you the truth, I didn't really put my heart into it. Not because I was thinking about the whole psychic thing. Please. That would make sense.

No, in spite of my resolve not to allow them to, my thoughts kept creeping back to Rob. Had he wondered where I was when I didn't show up for detention that afternoon? If he tried calling to find out where I was, he wouldn't be able to get through, since my dad had disconnected the phone. He had to have seen the paper, right? I mean, you would think, now that he knew I'd been touched by the finger of God, he might want to talk to me, right?

You would think that. But I guess not. Because

even though I listened for it, I never did hear the purr of that Indian.

And I don't think it was because the cops wouldn't let him through the blockade. I think he didn't even try.

So much for unrequited love. What is *wrong* with guys, anyway?

CHAPTER

12

When I woke up the next morning, I was kind of cranky, on account of Rob preferring not to have to go to jail rather than spend time in my company. But I perked up a little when I remembered I didn't have to slink around anymore, looking for a pay phone in order to call 1-800-WHERE-R-YOU. Hell, I could just call them from my own house. So I got up, reconnected the phone, and dialed.

Rosemary didn't answer, so I asked to speak to her. The lady who answered went, "Is this Jess?" and I said, "Yes, it is," and she said, "Hold on."

Only instead of connecting me with Rosemary, she connected me to Rosemary's butt-head supervisor, Larry, who I'd spoken to the day before. He went, "Jessica! What a pleasure. Thank you so much for calling. Do you have some more addresses for us today? I'm afraid we were cut off yesterday—"

"Yes, we were, Larry," I said, "thanks to your phoning in the Feds. Now, connect me with Rosemary, or I'm hanging up."

Larry sounded kind of taken aback. "Well, now, Jess," he said. "We didn't mean to upset you. Only, you have to understand, when we get a call like yours, we're obligated to investigate—"

"Larry," I said, "I understand perfectly. Now put Rosemary on the phone."

Larry made all these indignant noises, but, eventually, he transferred me to Rosemary. She sounded really upset.

"Oh, Jess," she said. "I am so sorry, honey. I wish I could have said something, warned you somehow. But you know, they trace all the calls—"

"That's okay, Rosemary," I said. "No harm done. I mean, what girl doesn't want a news crew from *Dateline* in her front yard?"

Rosemary said, "Well, at least you can joke about it. I don't know if I could."

"Water under the bridge," I said. At the time I really meant it, too. "So, look, here's the two kids from yesterday, and I have two more, if you're ready."

Rosemary was ready. She took down the information I gave her, said, "God bless you, sweetheart," and hung up. Then I hung up, too, and started getting ready for school.

Of course, that was easier said than done.

Outside our house it was a zoo again. There were more vans than ever before, some with these giant satellite dishes on top of them. There were reporters standing in front of them, and when I turned on the TV, it was sort of surreal, because on almost every channel, you could see my house, with someone standing there in front of it going, "I'm here in front of this quaint Indiana home, a home that has been declared a historic landmark by the county, but which has reached international fame by being home to heroine Jessica Mastriani, whose extraordinary psychic powers have led to the recovery of a half dozen missing children. . . ."

The cops were there, too. By the time I got downstairs, my mom was already bringing them seconds of coffee and biscotti. They were gulping them down almost as fast as she could bring them out.

And, of course, the minute I had put the phone down, it started ringing. When my dad picked it up, and someone asked to speak to me but wouldn't give his name, he disconnected it again.

It was, in other words, a mess.

None of us realized how bad a mess, however, until Douglas wandered into the kitchen, looking a little wild-eyed.

"They're after me," he said.

I nearly choked on my corn flakes. Because the only time Douglas ever starts talking about "them" is when he is having an episode.

My dad knew something was wrong, too. He put down his coffee and stared at Douglas worriedly.

Only my mom was oblivious. She was loading more biscotti onto a plate. She said, "Don't be ridiculous, Dougie. They're after Jessica, not you."

"No," Douglas said. He shook his head. "It's me they want. You see those dishes? Those satellite dishes on top of their vans? They're scanning my thought waves. They're using those satellite dishes to scan my thought waves."

I dropped my spoon. My dad went, gently, "Doug, did you take your medicine yesterday?"

"Don't you see?" Douglas, quick as a flash, yanked the biscotti out of my mom's hands and flung the plate to the floor. "Are you all blind? It's me they want! It's me!"

My dad jumped up and put his arms around Douglas. I pushed away my cereal bowl and said, "I better go. Maybe if I go, they'll follow me—"

"Go," my dad said.

I went. I got up, grabbed my flute and my backpack, and headed for the door.

They followed me. Or, I should say, they followed Ruth, who'd managed to convince the cops to let her out of her driveway and into mine. I jumped into the front seat, and we took off. If I hadn't been so worried about Douglas, I would have enjoyed watching all the reporters trying to scramble into their vans and follow us. But I was concerned. Douglas had been doing so well. What had happened?

"Well," Ruth said. "You have to admit, it's a lot to take."

"What is?"

Ruth reached up to adjust her rearview mirror. "Um," she said, staring pointedly into it. "That."

I looked behind us. We had a police escort, a bunch of the motorcycle cops rolling along beside us in an attempt to keep the hordes of news vans from bearing down on us too hard. But there were a lot more news vans than I would have thought. And they were all coming right at us. It wasn't going to be very funny when we tried to get out of the car.

"Maybe they won't let them onto school property," I said, hopefully.

"Yeah, right. Feeney's going to be standing there with a big welcome banner. Are you kidding?"

I said, "Well, maybe if I just talked to them . . ."

Which was how, just before the start of first period, I found myself standing on the school steps, fielding questions from these news reporters I'd been watching on TV my whole life.

"No," I said, in reply to one question, "it didn't hurt, really. It just felt sort of tingly."

"Yes," I said to someone else, "I do think the government should be doing more to find these children."

"No," I replied to another question, "I don't know where Elvis is."

Mr. Feeney, just as Ruth had predicted, was there all right. He was there with a little flock of reporters all his own. He and Mr. Goodhart stood on either side of me as I answered the reporters' questions. Mr. Goodhart looked uncomfortable, but Mr. Feeney, you could tell, was having the time of his life. He kept on saying to anyone who would listen how Ernest Pyle High School had won the state basketball championship in 1997. Like anyone cared.

And then, in the middle of this lame little impromptu press conference, something happened. Something happened that changed everything, even more than Douglas's episode had.

"Miss Mastriani," someone in the middle of the horde of reporters cried, "do you feel any guilt whatsoever over the fact that Sean Patrick O'Hanahan claims that, when his mother kidnapped him five years ago, it was in order to protect him from his abusive father?"

I blinked. It was another beautiful spring day, with the temperature already climbing into the seventies. But, suddenly, I felt cold.

"What?" I said, scanning the crowd, trying to figure out who was talking.

"And that your revealing Sean's whereabouts to the authorities," the voice went on, "has not only endangered his life, but put his mother's freedom in jeopardy?"

And then, instead of there being a sea of faces in front of me, there was only one face. I couldn't even tell if I was really seeing it, or if it was just in my mind's eye. But there it was, Sean's face, as I'd seen it that day in front of the little brick house in Paoli. A small face, white as paper, the freckles on it standing out like hives. His fingers, clinging to me, had shaken like leaves.

"Don't you tell anyone," he'd hissed at me. *"Don't you ever tell anyone you saw me, understand?"*

He had begged me not to tell. He had clung to me and begged me not to tell.

And I had told anyway. Because I had thought—I had honestly thought—he was being held against his will, by people of whom he was deathly afraid. He had certainly acted as if he were afraid.

And that was because he *had* been afraid. Of me.

I had truly thought I was doing the right thing. But I hadn't been doing the right thing. I hadn't done the right thing at all.

The reporters were still yelling questions at me. I heard them, but it was as if they were yelling them from very far away.

"Jessica?" Mr. Goodhart was looking down at me. "Are you all right?"

"I am not Sean Patrick O'Hanahan." That's what Sean had said to me that day outside his house. *"So you can just go away, do you hear? You can just go away."*

"And don't ever come back."

"Okay." Mr. Goodhart put his arm around me and started steering me back into the school. "That's enough for one day."

"Wait," I said. "Who said that? Who said that about Sean?"

But, unfortunately, as soon as they saw I was leaving, all the reporters started screaming questions at once, and I couldn't figure out who had asked me about Sean Patrick O'Hanahan.

"Is it true?" I asked Mr. Goodhart as he hustled me back inside the school.

"Is what true?"

"Is it true what that reporter said?" My lips felt funny, like I'd been to the dentist and gotten novocaine. "About Sean Patrick O'Hanahan not having been kidnapped at all?"

"I don't know, Jessica."

"Could his mom really go to jail?"

"I don't know, Jessica. But if it is, it isn't your fault."

"Why isn't it my fault?" He was walking me to my homeroom. For once I was late and nobody gave a damn. "How do you know it isn't my fault?"

"No court in the land," Mr. Goodhart said, "is going to award custody of a child to an abusive parent. The mother's probably just brainwashed the kid into thinking his father abused him."

"But how do you know?" I repeated. "How can anyone know? How am *I* supposed to know if what I'm doing, revealing these kids' locations to the authorities, is really in the best interest of the kids? I mean, maybe some of them don't want to be found. How am I supposed to know the difference?"

"You can't know," Mr. Goodhart said. We'd reached my classroom by then. "Jess, you can't know. You just have to assume that if someone loved them enough to report them missing, that person deserves to know where they are. Don't you think?"

No. That was the problem. I hadn't thought. I hadn't thought about anything at all. Once I'd figured out that my dream was true—that Sean Patrick O'Hanahan really was alive and well and living in that little brick house in Paoli—I had acted, without the slightest bit of further consideration.

And now, because of it, a little kid was in more trouble than ever.

Oh, yeah. I'd been touched by the finger of God, all right.

The question was, which finger?

CHAPTER

13

It wasn't all bad news.

The good news was, I no longer had detention.

Pretty impressive, right? Girl gets psychic powers, girl gets punishment lifted. Just like that. I wonder how Coach Albright would feel if he knew. Essentially, I'd pretty much gotten away with punching his star tackle. That's gotta be a kick in the pants, right?

In the midst of beating myself up over the whole Sean Patrick O'Hanahan thing, I spared a thought, every once in a while, for Miss Clemmings and the Ws. How was she going to handle Hank and Greg without my help? And what about Rob? Would he miss me? Would he even notice I was gone?

I got my answer after lunch. Ruth and I were

making our way toward our lockers, when suddenly she elbowed me, hard. I grabbed my side and was like, "What are you trying to do, give me a splenectomy? What is with you?"

She pointed. I looked. And then I knew.

Rob Wilkins was standing by my locker.

Ruth made a hasty and completely obvious retreat. I squared my shoulders and kept going. There was nothing to be nervous about. Rob and I were just friends, as he'd made only too clear.

"Hey," he said when I walked up.

"Hey," I said. I ducked my head, working my combination. Twenty-one, the age I'd like to be. Sixteen, the age I am. Thirty-five, the age I'll be before Rob Wilkins decides I am mature enough for him to go out with.

"So," he said. "Were you ever going to tell me?"

I got out my geometry book. "Actually," I said, "I wasn't planning on telling anyone."

"That's what I figured. And the kid?"

"What kid?" But I knew. I knew.

"The kid in Paoli. That was the first one?"

"Yep," I said. And all of a sudden I felt like crying.

Really. And I never cry.

Well, except for that time with the FBI agents in Mr. Goodhart's office.

"You could have told me," he said.

"I could have." I took out my geometry notebook. "Would you have believed me?"

"Yeah," he said. "Yeah, I would have."

I think he would have, too. Or maybe I just wanted to think he would have. He looked so . . . I don't know. Nice, I guess, standing there, leaning against the locker next door to mine. He didn't have any books or anything, just that ubiquitous paperback in the back pocket of his jeans, those jeans that were butter-soft from constant wear, and faded in spots, like at the knees and other, more interesting, places.

He had on a long-sleeved T-shirt, dark green, but he'd pushed up the sleeves so his forearms, tanned from all the riding he does, showed, and . . .

See how pathetic I am?

I slammed my locker door closed.

"Well," I said. "I gotta go."

"Jess," he called after me, as I was turning to walk away.

I looked back.

I changed my mind. That's what I was hoping he was going to say. *I changed my mind. Want to go to the prom with me?*

What he actually said was, "I heard. About the kid. Sean." He looked uncomfortable, like he wasn't used to having these kinds of conversations in the middle of the school hallway, under the unnatural glow of the fluorescent overheads.

But he went on anyway.

"It wasn't your fault, Jess. The way he acted that day, outside his house . . . well, I thought there was something weird going on with him, too. You couldn't have known. That's all." He nodded, like he was satisfied he'd made every point he'd meant to. "You did the right thing."

I shook my head. I could feel tears pricking my eyes. Dammit, I was standing there, with about a thousand people streaming around me, trying not to cry in front of this guy I had a total crush on. Could there possibly be anything more humiliating?

"No," I said. "I didn't."

And then I turned around and walked away.

And this time, he didn't try to stop me.

Since I didn't have detention anymore, Ruth and I came home together after school. We decided we'd practice together. She said she'd found a new concerto for flute and cello. It was modern, but we'd take a stab at it.

But when she pulled onto Lumley Lane, I saw right away something was wrong. All the reporters had been herded down to the far end of the street, where they were standing behind police barricades. When they saw Ruth's car, they started yelling and frantically taking pictures. . . .

But the cops wouldn't let them near our house.

When Ruth pulled into my driveway, and I saw the blood on the sidewalk, I knew why.

Not just on the sidewalk either, but little drops of it, leading all the way up to the front porch.

Ruth saw them, too. She went, "Uh-oh."

Then the screen door opened, and my dad and Mikey came out. My dad held up both his hands and said, "It's not as bad as it looks. This afternoon, Dougie attacked one of the reporters who'd stayed behind to try and interview the neighbors. They're both all right. Don't get upset."

I guess it might have sounded funny, my brother attacking a reporter. If it had been Mike who'd done it, it would have been very funny. But since it was Doug, it wasn't funny. It wasn't funny at all.

"Look," my dad said, sitting down on the porch steps. Ruth had switched off the ignition, and we both got out of the car. I went and sat down beside my dad, careful not to look at—or touch—any of the spots of blood all around us. Ruth went to sit with Mike on the porch swing. It creaked ominously under both their weights. Plus Mike looked annoyed at having to share it, only Ruth didn't notice.

"It's not your fault, Jess," my dad went on, "but the reporters, and the news vans, and the police and everything. It was all just a little too much for Dougie. Things started going a little haywire in his head. After you left this morning, we thought we'd calmed him down. We got him to take his medicine, and it seemed like he was okay. But the doctor says stress can sometimes—"

I groaned and laid my head upon my knees.

"What do you mean, it isn't my fault?" I wailed. "Of course it's my fault. Everything is my fault. If I'd never called that stupid number—"

"You had to call that stupid number," my dad said patiently. "If you hadn't called that stupid number, those kids' parents would still be wondering what happened to their little son or daughter—"

"Yeah," I said. "And Sean Patrick O'Hanahan wouldn't be being sent back to his abusive father. And his mother wouldn't be in trouble. And—"

"You did the right thing, Jess," my dad said again. "You can't know everything. And Douglas will be all right. It would just be better if he could be somewhere a little quieter—"

"Yeah, but where?" I demanded. "The hospital? Dougie has to go back to the hospital because of me? Nuh-uh. No, thanks, Dad. It's clear what the problem is here. The problem isn't Douglas." I took a deep breath. The air was thick and humid. Soon, I knew, it would be summer. It had grown steadily hotter all day, and now the late afternoon sun beat down on the porch.

Beat down on me.

"It's me," I said. "If I weren't here, Douglas would be all right."

"Now, honey," my dad said.

"No, I'm serious. If I weren't here, you wouldn't have reporters dropping Powerbar wrappers all over the lawn, and Mom wouldn't be baking biscotti twenty-four seven, and Douglas wouldn't be in the hospital—"

"Just what are you suggesting, Jessica?"

"You know what I'm suggesting. I think tomorrow I'd better do what Special Agent Johnson said, and go off to Crane for a while."

Both Ruth and Mike looked at me like I was nuts, but my dad said, after a moment's silence, "You have to do what you think is right, honey."

I said, "Well, I don't think it's right that this family should have to suffer because of me. And that's what we're doing, suffering. If I went away for a while, all those reporters and everything would go away. And then things could get back to normal. Maybe even Doug could come home."

Mike said softly, "Yeah, and maybe Claire would open her blinds back up. She's been so freaked by all the cameras—"

When Ruth and I turned to stare at him, he realized what he'd said, and clamped his mouth shut.

Ruth was the only person who voiced a note of dissent.

"I don't think that's a very good idea," she said. "Your going to Crane, I mean. I don't think that's a very good idea at all."

"Ruth," I said, surprised. "Come on. They just want to do some tests—"

"Oh, great," Ruth said. "So now you're a human guinea pig? Jess, Crane is an *Army* base. Get it? We're talking about the *military.*"

"Jeez, Ruth," I said. "Be a little paranoid, won't you? It'll be all right."

Ruth stuck out her chin. I don't know what it was. Maybe she'd just seen *Point of No Return* one too many times. Maybe she just didn't want to have to face the halls of Ernest Pyle High School on her own.

Or maybe she suspected something that I, even with my brand-new powers, couldn't sense. Ruth is smarter than most people . . . about some things, anyway.

"And what," she asked quietly, "if they want you to find more kids?"

My dad said, "Well, of course they'll want her to find more kids. That's what this is all about, I'm sure."

"Does Jess *want* to find more kids?" Ruth asked, her eyebrows raised.

They say that intelligence quotient tests only measure a certain kind of knowledge. Those of us who don't test well—for instance, me—comfort ourselves with the fact that, yeah, okay, Ruth has an IQ of 167, but she knows nothing about boys. Or yeah, Mike's 153, but again, what kind of people skills does the guy have? Nada.

But with that single question, Ruth proved there wasn't anything wrong with her people skills—at least, not where I was concerned. She'd hit the nail straight on the head.

Because there was no way I was finding any more missing kids. Not after Sean. Not unless I could be convinced the kids I was finding really wanted to be found.

Unlike Sean.

Mike went, "It doesn't matter what she wants. She has a moral obligation to the community to share this . . . whatever it is."

Ruth backed down at once. How could she take a stand against her beloved?

"You're right, Michael," she said, blinking at him shyly from behind her glasses.

So much for those people skills I mentioned.

"They're not going to make Jess do anything she doesn't want to," my dad said. "We're talking about the U.S. Government, here. Jessica is a citizen of the United States. Her constitutional rights are guaranteed. Everything will be all right."

And the sad thing is, at the time I really thought he was right.

I really and truly did.

CHAPTER

14

Crane Military Base, located about an hour's drive from my hometown, had been one of the many Army bases closed by the government during the eighties. At least, it was supposed to have closed. But, somehow, it never did—at least not all the way, in spite of all those stories in my hometown paper about all the locals who worked there as maintenance men and cooks who ended up losing their jobs. The military jets—the ones that were constantly breaking the sound barrier—never quite disappeared, and we still had uniformed officers showing up for lunch and dinner in all three of my dad's restaurants long after the base was said to have been shut down.

Douglas, when he was at his most paranoid, had insisted that Crane was like Area 51, that place where the Army swears there's no base, but over which people always see these flashing lights late at night.

But when I arrived at Crane, it certainly didn't look as if anyone was trying to keep the fact that it was still open a secret. And it didn't look as if it had been neglected, either. The place was pretty clean, the lawns neatly mowed, everything looking like it was in its place. I didn't see any giant hangars where spacecraft might have been hidden, but then again, they could have been keeping those underground, like in the movie *Independence Day*.

The first thing Special Agent Johnson did— after introducing me to Special Agent Smith, a lady officer with pretty pearl earrings who had apparently replaced his former partner, Special Agent Davies (out on disability . . . oops, my bad)—was show me and my dad the room in which I'd be staying—a nice room, actually, like a hotel room, with a TV and a phone and stuff. No soda fountain, I was relieved to see.

Then he and Special Agent Smith took us to a different building, where we met some Army guys, this one colonel who squeezed my hand too hard, and this pimply-faced lieutenant who kept looking at my jeans like they were thigh-high boots or something. Then the colonel introduced us to a bunch of doctors in a different building, who acted really excited to see me, and assured my dad I was in the best of hands. My dad, even though I knew he was itching to get back to his restaurants, wouldn't leave, in spite of the doctors' assurances. He kept saying stuff like, was Special Agent Smith going to be on call in case I needed something in the middle of the night, and who was going to make sure I got enough to eat? It was kind of embarrassing.

Finally, one of the doctors, whose nametag said Helen Shifton, told my dad they were ready for me, and that I'd call him as soon as I was back in my room. After that, it was sort of obvious that they wanted him gone, so my dad left, saying he'd be back to pick me up next week. By then, we hoped that all the hoopla with the reporters and everything would have died down, and I could come back home.

He hugged me right in front of everyone, and kissed the top of my head. I pretended not to like it, but after he left, I couldn't help feeling a little bit . . .

Well, scared.

I didn't tell that to Dr. Helen Shifton, though. When she asked how I was feeling, I said I was fine.

I guess she didn't believe me, though, since she and a nurse gave me this complete physical, and I mean complete, with blood drawn and stuff poked into me—the whole thing. They checked my blood pressure, my cholesterol, my heart, my throat, my ears, my eyes, the bottoms of my feet. They wanted to do a gynecological exam, so I let them, and while they were down there, I asked them about birth control and stuff . . . you know, because I might need some, someday, when I'm like forty.

Dr. Shifton was totally cool about it, unlike my family doctor would have been, and answered all my questions, and told me everything looked normal. She even examined my scar, the one the lightning had left, and said it looked as if it was fading, and that someday, it would probably go away altogether.

"When the scar goes, do the superpowers go, too?" I asked her, a little hopefully. Having superpowers was turning out to be more of a responsibility than I liked.

She said she didn't know.

After that, Dr. Shifton made me lie down in this big tube and keep really still while she took photographs of my brain. She told me not to think about anything, but I thought about Rob. I guess the pictures turned out okay anyway, since after that Dr. Shifton made me get dressed, and then she left and this little bald man came in and asked me a lot of really boring questions, like about my dreams and my sex life and stuff. Although my sex life had, in recent days, shown signs of improving—albeit all too briefly—I didn't really have anything to tell him, and my dreams were all pretty boring, too, mostly about forgetting how to play the flute right before my challenge with Karen Sue Hanky.

It wasn't until the little bald man started asking me a bunch of stuff about Douglas that I got annoyed. I mean, how did the U.S. Government know about Douglas's suicide attempt?

But they did, and when they asked me about it, I got defensive, and the little bald man wanted to know why.

So I said, "Wouldn't you be defensive if someone you didn't know started asking you stuff about your schizophrenic brother?" But he said no, he wouldn't—not unless he had something to hide.

So then I said the only thing I had to hide was the fact that I wanted to give him a big old knuckle sandwich, and he asked if I always felt so much aggression when discussing my family, and that's when I got up and left his office and told Dr. Shifton that I wanted to go home now.

You could tell Dr. Shifton was totally mad at the little bald man, but she couldn't show it, since she's a professional and all. She said to him that she thought we'd talked long enough, and he slunk away, giving me all these dirty looks, like I'd ruined his day or something. Then Dr. Shifton told me not to worry about him, that he was just a Freudian, and nobody thought much of him anyway.

After that, it was time for lunch. Special Agent Smith took me to the cafeteria, which was in yet another building. The food wasn't bad, better than at school. I had fried chicken and mashed potatoes. I noticed the little bald man eating there, too. He looked at what I was eating and wrote it down in a little book. I pointed this out to Special Agent Smith, and she told me to ignore him, he probably had a complex.

Since there was no one my age to sit with, I sat with Special Agent Smith, and asked her how she came to be an FBI agent. She was pretty cool, answering my questions. She said she was a distinguished expert in marksmanship, which I guess meant she was a good shot, but she'd never killed anyone. She'd pulled her gun on people plenty of times, though. She even took it out of the holster and showed it to me. It was cool, really heavy. I want one, but I'll wait until I'm eighteen.

Another thing I have to wait for until I'm eighteen.

After lunch, Dr. Shifton sent me into this other doctor's office, and we spent a boring half hour with him holding up playing cards with the backs facing me and asking me what suit they were. I was like, "I don't know. You're holding them away from me," and he told me to guess. I guessed right only about ten percent of the time. He said that was normal. I could tell he was disappointed, though.

Then this weird skinny lady tried to get me to move stuff with my mind. I felt so sorry for her; I really tried, but of course I failed miserably at that, too. Then she took me into a room that was like our language lab at school, and I got to wear headphones and I was kind of excited, thinking there'd be a movie.

But the doctor in charge, a very nervous-looking man, said there'd be no movie, just some photos. I was supposed to look at the photos, and that was all.

"Am I supposed to remember what these people look like?" I asked, after the doctor got the ball rolling and the photos started flashing up onto the screen in front of me. "Like is there going to be a quiz?"

He went, "No, no quiz."

"Then I don't see the point." I was already bored with looking at the pictures. The pictures were totally uninteresting. Just men, mostly white, some faintly Arab-looking. A few black. A few Asian. Some Hispanic. No names underneath, nothing. It was almost as boring as detention. Through the headphones came some piped-in Mozart—not very well-played, I might add. At least the flutist sucked. No life, you know?

After a while I took the headphones off and was like, "Can I take a break?"

Then the doctor got way nervous and asked if I had to go to the bathroom or something, and I wanted to be like, "No, this just blows," but I didn't want to insult his experiment, so I said, "I guess not," and I went back to looking at the photos.

Middle-aged white guy. Middle-aged white guy. Middle-aged Asian guy. Kind of hot-looking Arab guy, like that dude from *The Mummy*, only no facial tattoos. Middle-aged white guy. Middle-aged white guy. I wonder what they're serving for dinner. Old white guy. Serial-killer-looking kind of guy. Middle-aged white guy. Middle-aged white guy. Middle-aged white guy.

Finally, after what seemed like a year, Dr. Shifton came out and told me I'd done great, and that I could take the rest of the day off.

Actually, after that, there wasn't a whole lot of day left. It was around three o'clock. Back home, I'd just be going into detention. I felt a wave of homesickness. Can you believe that? I actually missed detention, Miss Clemmings, the Ws . . . and Rob, of course.

But when Special Agent Smith took me back to my room, and asked if I had a swimsuit, I forgot all about Rob, because it turned out there was a pool on the base. Since I hadn't brought a swimsuit, Special Agent Smith took me to a nearby mall, and I bought a kick-ass suit and a Sony PlayStation on the government's tab, and went back to the base and went swimming.

It was plenty hot out, and the sun was still coming down hard, even though it was so late in the day. I lounged around on a deck chair and watched the other people at the pool. It was mostly women with young children . . . the wives, I guessed, of the men who worked on the base.

Some of the older kids were playing Marco Polo. I leaned back on my deck chair and closed my eyes, feeling the sun burning my skin. It was a nice feeling. I started to relax.

Maybe, I told myself, everything would be all right after all. The smell of chlorine was tangy and pleasant in my nose. It smelled clean and sharp.

Things usually work out for the best.

The sound of the children shouting filled my ears. "Marco!" Then a splash.

"Polo!" Then another splash.

"Marco!" Splash.

"Polo!" Splash. Laughter.

"Marco!" Splash.

"Polo!" Splash. Screaming. Hysterical laughter.

I guess I must have fallen asleep, because I had a weird dream. In it, I was standing in an enormous body of water. All around me were kids. Hundreds and thousands of kids. Big kids. Little kids. Fat kids. Skinny kids. White kids. Black kids. Kids of every describable kind.

And they were all of them screaming "Polo," at me.

"Polo!" Splash. Scream.

"Polo!" Splash. Scream.

And I was swimming around, trying to catch them. Only in my dream, it wasn't just a game. I wasn't Marco. In my dream, if I didn't catch these kids, they would be swept away by these rapids, and tossed over the side of this like two-hundred-foot waterfall, and fall screaming to their deaths. Seriously.

So I was swimming and swimming, snatching up kid after kid, and moving them to safety, only to have them get caught in the current and get sucked away from me again. It was horrible. Kids were slipping past my fingertips, plunging to their deaths. And they weren't shouting "Polo" anymore, either. They were screaming my name. They were screaming my name as they died.

"Jess. Jess. Jessica, wake up."

I opened my eyes. Special Agent Smith was looking down at me. I was lying in a deck chair by the pool, but something was wrong. I was the only one there. All the mothers and their kids had gone home. And the sun was almost down. Just a last few rays lit the pool deck. And it had gotten quite a few degrees cooler outside.

"You fell asleep," Special Agent Smith said. "It looked like you were having a pretty bad dream. Are you okay?"

I said, "Yeah." I sat up.

Special Agent Smith handed me my T-shirt. "Ooo," she said, wincing. "You're all burnt. We should have gotten you some sunscreen."

I looked down at myself. I was the color of a mulberry.

"It'll turn to tan by tomorrow," I said.

"That must have been some dream. Do you want to tell me about it?"

"Not particularly."

After that, I went to my room and practiced my flute. I did the usual warm-up, then I practiced the piece Karen Sue Hanky had declared she was going to challenge me on. It was so damned easy, I started doing some improv, adding some trills here and there to jazz it up a little. When I got through, you could hardly recognize it was the same song. It sounded much better.

Poor Karen Sue. She's going to be stuck in fourth chair forever.

Then I did a little Billy Joel—"Big Shot," in honor of Douglas. He won't admit it, but it's his favorite.

I was cleaning my flute when someone tapped on the door. "Come in," I said, hoping it was room service. I was starved.

It wasn't, though. Room service, I mean. It was that colonel guy I'd met at the beginning of the day. Special Agents Smith and Johnson were with him, along with the nervous little doctor who'd made me look at all those pictures of middle-aged guys. He looked, for some reason, more nervous than ever.

"Hi," I said, when they'd all come in and were standing around, staring down at my flute like it was an AK-47 I was assembling or something. "Is it time for dinner?"

"Sure," Special Agent Johnson said. "Just let us know what you want."

I thought about it. Why not, I thought, ask for the best? "Surf and turf would be good," I said.

"Done," the colonel said, and he nodded at Special Agent Smith. She took out her cell phone and punched some numbers, then spoke softly into it. God, I thought. How sexist. Here Special Agent Smith is, an FBI agent, who put herself through school and is a distinguished expert markswoman and all, and she still has to take the food orders.

Remind me not to be an FBI agent when I grow up.

"Now," the colonel said. "I was told you had a little nap today."

I was bending over, putting the different pieces of my flute in their individual sections in the velvet-lined case. But something in the colonel's voice made me look up at him.

He, like all the guys in the photos, was middle-aged, and he was white. He had what they call in the books we are forced to read in English class "ruddy features," meaning he looked as if he spent a lot of time outdoors. Not tan, like me, but sun-damaged and wrinkly. He had bright blue eyes, however. He squinted down at me and went, "You wouldn't, during your little nap, happen to have dreamed about any of those men whose photos you saw today in Dr. Leonard's office, now, did you, Miss Mastriani?"

I blinked. What was going on here?

I looked at Special Agent Smith. She had hung

up her cell phone, and now she looked at me expectantly.

"You remember, Jessica," she said. "You told me you had a bad dream."

"Yeah," I said, slowly. I think I was starting to catch on. "So?"

"So I mentioned it to Colonel Jenkins," Special Agent Smith said. "And he was just wondering if you happened to dream about any of the men whose photos you saw this afternoon."

I said, "No."

Dr. Leonard nodded and said to the colonel, "It's just as we suspected. REM-stage sleep is necessary for the phenomenon to occur, Colonel. Nappers rarely achieve the level of deep sleep necessary for REM."

Colonel Jenkins frowned down at me. "So you think tomorrow morning then, Leonard?" he rumbled. He looked very forbidding in his uniform, with all its medals and pins. He must, I thought, have fought in some pretty important battles.

"Oh, definitely, sir," Dr. Leonard said. Then he looked down at me and went, in his nervous little voice, "You tend only to have these, er, dreams about the missing children after a complete night of rest, am I correct, Miss Mastriani?"

I went, "Uh. Yeah. I mean, yes."

Dr. Leonard nodded. "Then we should check back with her tomorrow morning, sir."

Colonel Jenkins said, "I don't like it," so loudly that I jumped. "Smith?"

"Sir?" Special Agent Smith snapped to attention.

"Bring the photos," he said. "Bring them for her to look at tonight, before she goes to sleep. So they'll be fresh in her memory."

"Yes, sir," Special Agent Smith said. Then she got back on the cell phone and started murmuring things into it again.

Colonel Jenkins looked down at me. "We have high hopes for you, young lady," he told me.

I went, "You do?"

"We do, indeed. There are hundreds of men— traitors to this great nation—who have been running from the law for far too long. But now that we have you, they don't stand a chance. Do they?"

I didn't know what to say.

"Do they?" he barked.

I jumped and said, "No, sir."

Colonel Jenkins seemed to like the sound of that. He left, along with Dr. Leonard and Special Agents Smith and Johnson. A little while later, this guy in a chef's uniform delivered shrimp scampi and a perfectly grilled steak to my door.

I wasn't fooled. There may not have been a soda fountain in my room, but I knew what was going on. The book of photos arrived shortly after the food did. I flipped through it while I ate, just for the hell of it. Traitors, Colonel Jenkins had said. Were these men spies? Murderers? What? Some of them looked pretty scary. Others didn't.

What if they weren't murderers or spies? What if they were just people who, like Sean, had gotten into some trouble through no fault of their own? Was it really *my* responsibility to find them?

I didn't know. I thought I'd better talk to somebody who might.

So I called my house. My mom answered. She told me that Dougie had been released from the hospital, and that he was doing so much better now that he was back in his own room and "all the excitement had died down."

All the excitement, I knew, had moved to the gates outside of Crane, where all the news vans and stuff had gone as soon as they learned I'd been brought there. Even so, my mom kept complaining about how the whole thing had been triggered by Dad making Dougie work in the restaurant, until finally I couldn't stand it anymore, and I said, "That's bullshit, Mom, it was because of me and all the reporters," and then she got mad at me for swearing, so I hung up without having talked to my dad—which was who I'd called to talk to in the first place.

To cheer myself up, I started flipping around the channels on my big TV. I watched *The Simpsons*, and then a movie about some boys who do a beauty makeover on this girl who looked just fine before they got their mitts on her. This movie was so boring—although Ruth would have liked it, because of the beauty makeover thing—that I started flipping again. . . .

And then froze when I got to CNN . . .

Because they were showing a picture of me.

It wasn't my dorky school picture. It was a picture one of the reporters must have taken when I wasn't looking. In the picture, I was laughing. I wondered what I'd been laughing at. I couldn't remember laughing too much these past few days.

Then my picture was replaced by another one I recognized. Sean. A picture of Sean Patrick O'Hanahan, looking much as I'd last seen him, baseball cap turned around backwards, his freckles standing out starkly from his face.

I turned up the volume.

"—irony is that the boy appears to be missing *again*," the reporter said. "Authorities say Sean disappeared from his father's Chicago home yesterday before dawn, and he hasn't been seen, or heard from, since. It is believed that the boy left of his own volition, and that he is heading back to Paoli, Indiana, where his mother is being held without bail on charges of kidnapping and endangering the welfare of a minor—"

Oh, my God. They'd *arrested* Sean's mom. They'd arrested Sean's mom, because of *me*. Because of what *I'd* done.

And now the kid was on the lam. And it was all my fault. I'd been lounging around a pool while Sean was God knew where, going through God knew what, trying to get back to his incarcerated mother. And just what, I wondered, did he think he was going to do when he got back to Paoli? Bust her out of jail?

The kid was alone and hopeless, because of me.

Well, all that was going to change, I decided, switching off the TV. He may have been alone for now, but come tomorrow, he wouldn't be. Want to know why?

Because I was going to find him again.

I had done it once. I could do it again.

And this time, I was going to do it right.

CHAPTER

15

When they came for me the next morning, I was already gone.

Oh, don't get your panties in a wad. I left a note. It went like this:

> To Whom It May Concern,
> I had to run out to do an errand. I'll be right back.
> Sincerely,
> Jessica Mastriani

I mean, I didn't want anyone to worry.

What happened was, I woke up early. And when I woke up, I knew where Sean was. Again.

So I showered and got dressed, and then I went out into the hallway, down some stairs, and out a door.

No one tried to stop me. No one was even around,

except some soldiers, who were practicing drills or something in the yard. They just ignored me.

Which suited me fine.

Yesterday, when I'd been coming back from the pool, I'd noticed a little minibus that had pulled up to a stop outside the base's family housing units, where the officers with spouses and children lived. I walked over there now. Again, nobody tried to stop me. After all, it wasn't like I was a prisoner, or anything.

The minibus, the people at the stop said, went into the nearest town, where I'd bought my swimsuit and Sony PlayStation . . . and where I happened to know there was a bus station.

So I waited with all the other people, and when the minibus finally pulled up, I got on it. It chugged away, right in front of all the news vans and reporters and stuff. It rolled right along past them and the soldiers guarding the entrance to the base, keeping the reporters out.

And as simple as that, I left Crane Military Base.

The town outside of Crane isn't exactly this booming metropolis, but I still had trouble finding the bus station. I had to ask three people. First the minibus driver, who gave me the lamest directions on earth, then the kid behind the cash register of a convenience mart, and finally an old guy sitting outside a barber shop. In the end, I located it thanks to the fact that there was a bus sitting outside of it.

I bought my round-trip ticket—seventeen dollars—with the money my dad had given me before he'd left. "In case of an emergency," he'd said, and slipped me a hundred bucks.

Well, this was an emergency. Sort of.

I had breakfast at the bus stop. I got two chocolate fudge Pop-Tarts and a Sprite from the vending machines. Another dollar seventy-five.

I figured I might be bored during my ride, so I bought a book to read. It was the same book I'd noticed in Rob's back pocket the last time I'd seen him. I thought reading the same book might somehow bring us closer together.

Okay, I admit it: that's not true. It was the only book on the rack that looked the least bit interesting.

My bus pulled up at nine o'clock. I was the only person who got on it. I got a window seat. Have you ever noticed that things always look better when you look at them out of one of those tinted bus windows? I'm serious. Then you get off the bus and everything's all bright and you can see the dirt and you just think, "Ugh."

That's what I think, anyway.

It took us more than an hour to get to Paoli. I spent most of it looking out the window. There's not a lot to see in Indiana, except cornfields. I'm sure that's true of most states, however.

When we got to Paoli, I got off the bus and went into the station. It was bigger than the one outside of Crane. There were rows of plastic chairs for people to sit in, and a bank of pay phones. Still, I could pick out the undercover cops easy. There was one sitting by the vending machines, and another sitting near the men's room. Every time a bus came in, they'd stand up and go outside, and pretend to be waiting for someone. Then, when Sean didn't get off the bus, they'd go back and sit down again.

I observed them for over an hour, so I know what I'm talking about. There was also an unmarked police car parked across the street from the bus station, and another one in front of the bowling alley, a little ways away.

When it came time for Sean's bus to arrive, I knew I had to set up a diversion so the cops wouldn't snatch Sean before I had a chance to talk to him. So this is what I did:

I started a fire.

I know. People could have been killed. But listen, I made sure no one was in there first. I just lit this match I got from a pack I found, and threw it into the trash can in the ladies' room, after first checking to make sure all the stalls were empty. Then I went and stood by the pay phones, like I was expecting a call. Nobody noticed me. Nobody ever notices me. Short girls like me, we don't exactly stand out, you know?

After a few minutes, the smoke was billowing out really good. One of the ticket sellers noticed it first. She went, "Oh, my God! Fire! Fire!" and pointed toward the ladies' room door.

The other clerks totally freaked out. They started screaming for everyone to get out. Somebody shouted, "Dial 911!" One of the undercover cops asked if there was a fire extinguisher anywhere. The other got on his cell phone. He was telling the guys waiting outside in the unmarked cars to radio the fire department.

And right then the eleven-fifteen from Indianapolis pulled up outside. I sauntered out to meet it.

Sean was the fifth person to get off. He had on a disguise—or what he thought was one, anyway. What he'd done was, he'd dyed his hair brown. Big deal. You could still see his freckles from a mile away. Plus he still had on that stupid Yankees cap. At least he'd tried to pull it down low over his face.

But, I'm sorry, a twelve-year-old kid, who was small for his age anyway, getting off a Greyhound by himself, in the middle of a school day? Talk about conspicuous.

Fortunately, my little fire was really plugging away. I don't know if you've ever smelled burning plastic trash can before, but let me tell you, it isn't pleasant. And the smoke? Pretty black. Everyone who got off the bus looked, in a startled way, toward the station. Thick, acrid smoke was really pouring out of it now. All the ticket-takers were standing around outside, talking in shrill voices. You could tell this was the most exciting thing that had happened in the Paoli bus station for a while. The undercover cops were rushing around, trying to make sure everybody had gotten out. And then the fire engines showed up, sirens on full blast.

While all this was going on, I stepped up to Sean, took him by the arm, and said, "Keep moving," and started steering him down this alley by the station, as fast as I could.

He didn't want to come with me at first. It was kind of hard to hear what he said, since the fire engine's siren was so loud. I shouted into his ear, "Well, if you'd prefer to go with them, they're over there waiting for you," and I guess he got the message, because he stopped struggling after that.

When we'd gotten far enough away from the station that the sound of the sirens could no longer drown out our voices, Sean snatched his arm out of my grasp and demanded, in a very rude voice, "What are *you* doing here?"

"Saving your butt," I said. "What were you thinking, coming back here? This is the first place anybody with brains would look for you, you know."

Sean's blue eyes flashed at me from beneath the brim of his baseball cap. "Yeah? Well, where else am I supposed to go? My mom's in the city lockup," he said. "Thanks to *you.*"

"If you had leveled with me that day," I said, "instead of acting like such a little head-case, none of this would be happening."

"No," Sean shot back. "If you weren't a *nark*, none of this would be happening."

"Nark?" That got me mad. Everyone had been going on about what a wonderful "gift" I had. How it was a miracle, a blessing, blah, blah, blah.

No one had ever called me a *nark.*

Little brat, I thought. Why am I even wasting my time? I should just leave him here. . . .

But I couldn't. I knew I couldn't.

I walked on without saying a word. It wasn't very pleasant, the alley we were in. There were Dumpsters brimming with trash on either side of us, and broken glass beneath our feet. Even worse, in about five yards, the alley ended, and I could see there was a busy street up ahead. If I was going to make sure Sean wasn't caught, I had to keep him from being seen.

"Anyway," Sean said, in the same snotty voice, "if anybody with a brain knew I'd be coming here, how come none of them found me?"

"Because I'm the only one who knew which bus you'd be coming in on," I said.

"How'd you know that?"

I gave him a bored look. He said, in a very sarcastic way, "You *dreamed* I'd be on the eleven-fifteen from Indianapolis?"

"Hey. Nobody said my dreams were interesting."

"Well, so what was all that about back there? You said *they* were waiting for me. Who's *they?*"

"Bunch of undercover cops posted in the bus

station, waiting for you. They must have suspected that was how you'd try to get here. By bus, I mean. I had to create a diversion."

His blue eyes grew wide. "*You* started that fire?"

"Yeah." We were almost to the street. I put my arm out and stopped him. "Look, we have to talk. Where can we go around here where we can . . . you know, blend?"

"I don't want to talk to you," he said. He sounded like he meant it, too.

"Yeah, well, you're going to. Somebody has to get you out of this mess."

"And you think *you're* going to do it?" he asked with a sneer.

"Like it or not, Junior," I said, "I'm all you've got."

That earned me an eye-roll. Well, it was progress, anyway.

We ended up going where everybody goes when they don't know where else to go.

That's right: the mall.

The mall in Paoli, Indiana, is no Mall of America, let me tell you. It was two stories, all right, but there were only about twenty stores, and the food court consisted of a Pizza Hut and an Orange Julius. Still, beggars can't be choosers. And since it was lunchtime, at least we weren't the only kids around. Apparently, the sole place in Paoli where it was possible to get a pitcher and a pie was the Pizza Hut in the mall, so the place was jammed with high school kids, trying to squeeze a meal into the fifty minutes they had before they had to get back to campus.

I told Sean to try to sit up tall in his seat. I was hoping he could pass, maybe, for a scrawny freshman.

And that I could pass for a loser who'd date a freshman.

"Whoa," I said, as I watched him attack his pizza. "Slow down. What, is that the first thing you've eaten all day?"

"Two days," he said, with his mouth full.

"What is wrong with you? You didn't think to steal any money from your dad before you took off?"

He said, chugging down a few swallows of Pepsi, "A credit card."

"Oh, a credit card. Smart. It's easy to buy stuff at McDonald's with a credit card."

"I just needed the bus ticket from Chicago," he said defensively.

"Oh, right." So that was how the cops knew he'd be there. "But no food."

"I forgot about food," he said. "Besides." He gave me this look. I can't really describe it. I guess it was the kind of look you would call reproachful. "I was too worried about my mom to eat."

I'll admit it. I fell for it. I got all weepy for him, and kicked myself for like the hundredth time.

Then I saw the size of the bite he took out of his last piece of pizza.

"Oh, cut the crap," I said. "I said I was sorry."

"No, you didn't."

"I didn't?" I blinked at him. "Okay, well, I'm sorry. That's why I'm here. I want to help you."

Sean shoved his empty plate at me. "Help me to another pizza," he said. "This time, no vegetables."

I sat there and watched him down a second individual pizza. I was only having a soda. I can't eat Pizza Hut. Not because it's gross or anything. I'm sure it's very good. Only we've never been allowed to eat pizza from anywhere but our own restaurants. Both my parents treat it like this huge betrayal if you even *think* about Little Caesar's, or Dominos, or whatever. It was a pie from Mastriani's, or nothing.

So I was having nothing. It's not easy, having parents in the restaurant business.

"So," I said, when Sean seemed well enough into the second pie for conversation. "What, exactly, were you planning on doing when you got here?"

He looked at me darkly. "What do you think?"

"Busting your mother out of jail? Oh, sure. Good plan."

His dark look turned into a glower. "You did it," he pointed out, and there was admiration in his voice. Grudging, but there just the same. "With the fire in the bus station. I could do something like that."

"Oh, yeah. And all the guards would come

rushing outside, and leave all the jail cells open, and you could just sneak in and grab your mom and go."

"Well," he said. "I didn't say I actually had a plan. Yet. But I'll come up with something. I always do."

"Well," I said. "I think I have one."

He just looked at me. "One what?"

"A plan."

"Aw, Jesus," he said, and reached for his Pepsi.

"Hey," I said. "Don't swear."

He looked at me very sarcastically. "You do it."

"I do not. And, besides, I'm sixteen."

He rolled his eyes again. "Yeah, that makes you an adult, I guess. Do you even have a driver's license?"

I fiddled with my straw. He had me there. I had my learner's permit, of course, but I had sort of accidentally flunked my first try at the driving test. It wasn't my fault, of course. Something weird seems to happen when I get behind a wheel. It all goes back to that speed thing. If no one else is on the road, why should you only go thirty-five?

"Not yet," I said. "But I'm working on it."

"Jesus." Sean flopped his eighty-pound body against the back of the booth. "Look, you are not exactly trustworthy, you know? You busted me once already, remember?"

"That was a mistake," I said. "I said I was

sorry. I bought you pizza. I told you I have a plan to make things right again. What more do you want?"

"What more do I want?" Sean leaned forward so that the cheerleaders at the next table wouldn't overhear him. "What I want is for things to go back the way they were before you came along and severely messed them up."

"Oh, yeah? Well, no offense, Sean, but I don't think things were exactly swell before. I mean, what's going to happen when one of your teachers, or your friends' moms, or your Boy Scout leader, goes to the grocery store and sees your face on the back of a milk carton, huh? Are you and your mom going to pick up and run every time someone recognizes you? Are the two of you going to keep running until you're eighteen? Is that the plan?"

Sean eyed me angrily from beneath the brim of his baseball cap. "What else are we supposed to do?" he demanded. "You don't know . . . My dad, he's got friends. That's why the judge ruled the way he did. My dad got his friends to put the squeeze on the guy. He knew exactly what kind of guy my dad is. But he awarded him custody anyway. My mom didn't have a chance. So, yeah, we'll keep running. No one can help us."

"You're wrong," I said. "I can."

Sean leaned forward and said, very deliberately, "You . . . can't . . . even . . . drive."

"I know that. But I can help you. Listen to me.

My best friend's dad is a lawyer, a good one. Once, when I was over at their house, I heard him talking about this case where a kid sued to be emancipated—"

"This," Sean said, shoving his empty plate away, "is bullshit. I don't know why I'm even listening to you."

"Because I'm all you've got. Now, listen—"

"No," Sean said, shaking his head. "Don't you get it? I've heard about you."

I blinked at him. "What are you talking about?"

"I saw on the news how they've got you up at that place, that military base."

"Yeah? So?"

"You're so stupid," Sean said. "You don't know anything. I bet you don't even know why they got you there. Do you?"

I shifted uncomfortably in my seat. "Sure, I do. They're doing some experiments on me. You know, to figure out how it is I know where people like you are. That's all."

"That isn't *all*. They've got you lookin' for people, don't they?"

I thought about those photos, all those middle-aged men it had seemed so important to the colonel for me to look at.

"Maybe . . ."

"So, don't you get it? You're not helping anybody. You don't know who those guys were. Some of those people they want you to find might be on the run for a reason, like me and my mom. Some of them might actually be innocent. And you're servin' 'em up to the cops like big old plates of chocolate-glazed donuts."

I don't like to hear the police disparaged, especially by someone so young. After all, the police provide a vital service for our society, for little pay and even less glory. I said, my voice sounding lame even to my own ears, "I am sure that if someone is wanted by the U.S. Government, he must be guilty of something. . . ."

But the truth was, he wasn't saying anything I hadn't already thought of myself. For some reason, he reminded me of my dream. *Marco. Polo. Marco. Polo.* So many people, so many voices.

And I couldn't reach a single one of them.

Sean's face was white beneath his freckles. "What about *The Fugitive*, huh? He hadn't done anything. It was that one-armed man. For all you know, one of those people they want you to find for them might be just like Harrison Ford in that movie. And you're Tommy Lee Jones." He shook his head disgustedly. "You really are a nark, you know that?"

Nark? Me? I wanted to wring the little twerp's neck. I was totally regretting having come after him like this.

Marco.

"Nark's not even the word for it," he said. "You know what you are? A dolphin."

I gaped at him. Was he kidding? Dolphins were friendly, intelligent animals. If he was trying to insult me, he'd have to try a little harder.

"You know what the government used to do?" Sean was on a roll. "They used to train dolphins to swim up to boats and tap them with their noses. Then, when World War I started, they strapped bombs to the dolphins' backs, and made them swim up to enemy boats and touch them with their noses. But this time when they did it, what do you think happened? The bombs went off, and the enemy ships—and the dolphins—were blown to smithereens. Oh, sure, everybody says, 'Think how many people would have been killed by that boat, if it hadn't been blown up. The dolphin gave its life for a worthy cause.' But I bet the *dolphin* didn't feel that way. The dolphin didn't start the war. The dolphin had nothing to do with it."

He narrowed his eyes at me. "Do you know what, Jess?" he said. "You're the dolphin now. And it's just a matter of time before they blow you up."

I narrowed my eyes right back at him, but I had to admit, the story about the dolphins gave me the chills.

Polo.

"I'm no dolphin," I said. I was beginning to regret having found Sean Patrick O'Hanahan. And I definitely regretted having bought him two individual pizzas and a large Pepsi.

Unfortunately, though, the more I thought

about it, sitting there in the restaurant, with the Paoli High cheerleaders giggling in the next booth, and the mall Muzac playing softly around us, the more I realized that was exactly what I was . . . or rather, what I'd almost let myself become. *I'll be right back.* That's what I'd said in the note I'd left that morning. Had I really meant that? Had I really meant to come back?

Or had I actually meant hasta la vista, baby, this tuna is dolphin-free?

Marco.

"Look," I said to Sean. "We aren't here to discuss my problems. We're here to discuss yours."

He eyed me. "Fine," he said. "What am I supposed to do?"

"In the first place," I said, "stop using your dad's credit card. Here." I dug around in my pocket, then pushed what was left of my dad's hundred dollars at him. "Take this. Then we're going to get you into a cab."

"A cab?"

"Yeah, a cab. You can't go back to the bus station, and we've got to get you out of Paoli. I want you to go to my school—" I'd reached into my backpack and brought out a pen. I was scrawling the address of Ernest Pyle High School on a Pizza Hut napkin. "Ask for Mr. Goodhart. Tell him I sent you. He'll help you. Tell him he needs to call Ruth's dad, Mr. Abramowitz. Here, I'm writing it down for you. Quit grabbing my hand, I'm writing it down for you."

But Sean kept on pawing at my hand. I didn't know what the kid wanted. The pen? What did he want the pen for?

"Cool it, would you?" I said, looking up at him. "I'm writing as fast as I can."

But then I got a look at his face. He wasn't even looking at me. He was looking just past me, at the door to the restaurant.

I turned around, just in time to make eye contact with Colonel Jenkins. When he saw me, his big hands balled up into fists, and I was reminded, inexplicably, of Coach Albright.

And that wasn't all. Marching behind him was a whole pack of meaty-fisted guys in army fatigues and crew cuts, who just happened to be armed.

Polo.

"Shit," I said.

The colonel nodded at me. "There she is," he said.

Sean may only have been twelve, but he sure wasn't stupid. He whispered, "Run!"

And even though he was only twelve, that sounded like pretty good advice to me.

CHAPTER

16

Colonel Jenkins and his men were blocking the doorway, but that was okay. There was a side door that had the word *Exit* over it. We dove through it, and found ourselves right in front of JCPenney.

"Wait," I said to Sean as he was preparing to flee. I had had the presence of mind to hang on to the napkin I'd written on. I reached out and grabbed him by his shirt collar, then shoved the napkin in the front pocket of his jeans. He looked a little surprised.

"Now go," I said, and shoved him.

We split up. We didn't discuss it or anything. It just happened. Sean took off toward the Photo Hut. I headed for the escalators.

Back when I'd first started having to defend Douglas at school, and I hadn't known too much about fighting, my dad had taken me aside and given me a few pointers. One of the best pieces of advice he gave me—besides showing me how to hit—was that if I ever found myself in a situation where I was outnumbered, the best thing to do was run. And, specifically, run downhill. Never, my father said, go uphill—or stairs, or whatever—during a chase. Because if you go up, and the people after you block the only way down, you have no way of getting out—except by jumping.

But I had Sean to think about. Seriously. Thanks to me, there were armed men chasing us, for Christ's sake. I was not going to let them get hold of a little twelve-year-old kid, a kid who'd only gotten involved in this in the first place through my own fault.

So I knew that I was going to have to let myself get caught in the end . . . but, in the meantime, I had to make this chase last as long as possible, in order to give Sean a solid chance at escaping. I was going to have to create another diversion. . . .

And so I headed for those escalators.

And, by God, they followed me right up them.

It was still lunchtime so, except for the food court, the mall wasn't that crowded. But what few people there were I managed to weave around pretty good. The soldiers chasing after me weren't quite so nimble: I heard people screaming as they tried to get out of the way, and things like a vending cart called the Earring Tree, which I whizzed by with no problem, crashed to the floor as the soldiers stumbled into it.

I knew better than to dive into any stores in my efforts to ditch these guys. They'd just corner me there. I kept to the main corridor, which had plenty of stuff to dodge around—a big fountain, cookie vendors, and, best of all, a giant traveling diorama, featuring life-size robotic dinosaurs, meant to teach kids and their parents about pre-historic earth.

I am not kidding. Well, okay, maybe about the life-size part. The tallest dinosaur was only about twenty feet tall, and that was the *T. Rex.* But they were all crowded into this hundred-foot space, jammed in there with fake ferns and palm trees and jungly-type stuff. Weird jungle sounds, like shrieking monkeys and birds, played over these speakers designed to look like rocks. There was even, in one area, a volcano from which actual fake lava was spewing—or made to look like it was spewing, anyway.

I looked behind me. My pursuers had untangled themselves from the mess by the Earring Tree, and were now gaining on me. I glanced to my side, over the balustrade that looked out across the main floor, a story below me. I saw Sean dodging past Baskin-Robbins, Colonel Jenkins close at his heels.

"Hey," I yelled.

Heads everywhere whipped around as people turned to stare at me, including Colonel Jenkins.

"Here I am!" I shouted. "Your new dolphin! Come and get me!"

Colonel Jenkins, as I had hoped, stopped chasing Sean and headed for the escalator.

I, of course, headed for the dinosaur diorama.

I hurdled across the velvet rope separating the display from the rest of the mall, followed closely by a half dozen of Colonel Jenkins's men. As my sneakered feet sank into the brown foamy stuff they'd sprayed on the mall floor to look like dirt, I was assaulted by the sound of jungle drums—apparently the makers of the diorama were unaware that dinosaurs predated man (and drums) by several hundred thousand years. There was a lonely wail, which sounded mysteriously like a peacock to me. Then a roar—distinctly lion—and steam sprayed from the *T. Rex*'s nostrils, two dozen feet above my head.

I dodged behind a couple of velociraptors, who were feasting on the bloody carcass of a saber-toothed tiger. No good. Jenkins's men were on my heels. I decided to really screw with them, and leapt into the shallow water they'd set up to look like a lake, out of which both the fake volcano and the head of a brachiosaurus reared. I sank into the artificially blue water, the water hitting me about mid-shin, soaking my sneakers and the bottoms of my jeans.

Then I started wading.

Jenkins's men, apparently thinking that catching me was not exactly worth getting their feet wet, halted on the rim of the artificial lake.

Okay, so I knew they were going to catch me eventually. I mean, come on. Even if I got out of the mall, where was I going to go? Home?

Not.

But I didn't have to make it easy on them. So, when I saw them elbow each other and split up to opposite sides of the lake, ready to catch me wherever I tried to come ashore, I did the only thing I could think of:

I climbed the volcano.

Okay, my sneakers were kind of squelchy. And okay, the volcano wasn't all that sturdy, and groaned beneath my weight. But hey, I had to do something.

And when I reached the top of the volcano, it was just in time for it to start spewing again. I stood up there—some fifteen feet in the air—and looked down at everyone, as all around me steam hissed out, and the lava, made of scarlet plastic with a bunch of little lights inside it, started to glow. The diorama's bogus sound track made a noise like the earth splitting, and then a thunderous rumble shook the so-called lake.

"Be careful!" shouted an old lady in jogging shoes, who'd watched from the velvet rope as I'd climbed.

"Don't slip in those wet shoes, dear," cried her friend.

The soldiers looked at them almost as disgustedly as I did.

From my perch, I could see down to the mall's main floor. As I watched, another six soldiers stormed by—and as soon as they passed, Sean darted out from between some racks of clothes in the Gap and headed, a streak of blue jeans and badly dyed brown hair, toward the Cineplex.

I knew a secondary diversion was necessary. So I teetered on the rim of the volcano and shouted, "Don't come any closer, or I'll jump!"

Both the old ladies gasped. The soldiers looked more disgusted than ever. In the first place, they'd clearly had no intention of coming any closer. In the second, even if I did jump, that fall wouldn't exactly be fatal: I wasn't all that high up.

Still, I suppose it looked very dramatic. There I was, this young virgin (unfortunately), poised on the edge of a volcano. Too bad my hair was so short, and I wasn't dressed in flowing white. Jeans spoiled the effect, in my opinion.

Then Colonel Jenkins strode up, pointing at me and bleating at his soldiers in a manner that more than ever put me in mind of Coach Albright.

"What's she doin' up there?" he demanded. "Get her down right now."

I glanced down at the Cineplex. I could still see Sean, cowering behind a life-size cardboard cutout of Arnold Schwarzenegger. The soldiers were milling around, trying to figure out where he'd disappeared to.

Hoping to get their attention long enough for Sean to be able to make another run for it, I shouted, "I really mean it! If anyone comes near me, I'll do it! I'll jump!"

Bingo. The soldiers looked up. Sean slithered out from behind the cardboard Arnold and made a break for the concession stand.

"All right, Miss Mastriani," Colonel Albright called out to me. "Fun's over. You come down here right now before you hurt yourself."

"No," I said.

Colonel Jenkins sighed. Then he flicked a finger, and four of his men climbed over the velvet rope and began wading toward me.

"Get back," I cried warningly. Sean, I could see, had only to duck past the ticket-taker, and he'd be in. "I mean it!"

"Miss Mastriani," Colonel Jenkins said, in a tone of voice that suggested to me that he was trying very hard to be reasonable. "Have we done something to offend you? Have you been mistreated in any way since your father left you in our care?"

"No," I said. The soldiers were coming closer.

"Isn't it true, in fact, that Dr. Shifton and Special Agent Smith and everyone else at Crane have gone out of their way to make you feel comfortable and welcome?"

"Yes," I said. Below, the ticket-taker caught

Sean trying to sneak into the theater. She grabbed him by his shirt collar, and said something I couldn't hear.

"Well, then, let's be rational. You come on back to Crane, and we'll talk this out."

The ticket-taker raised her voice. The six soldiers watching me started to turn their heads, distracted by the commotion at the Cineplex.

I looked at the two old ladies. "Call the police," I shouted. "I'm about to be taken against my will back to Crane Military Base."

"Crane," the old lady in the jogging shoes said. "Oh, but that's closed."

"Goddammit," Colonel Jenkins said, apparently forgetting his audience. "Come down from there right now, or I'll pull you down myself!"

Both of the old ladies gasped. But the soldiers had spied Sean. They began jogging toward him.

And the soldiers Colonel Jenkins had sicced on me were almost at the base of my volcano.

"Oh, nuts," I said as I watched Sean get nabbed. That was it. It was over.

But there was no reason to make it easy on them.

"Let the kid go," I threatened, "or I'll jump!"

"Don't do it, honey," one of the old ladies shouted. They had been joined now by some of the high school kids, who'd come out to see what all the commotion was.

The high school kids yelled at me to jump.

I looked beneath me, down into the center of

the volcano. I could see a circle of bare mall floor there, ringed by bars of metal scaffolding, which was holding the volcano up. They'd drag me out, of course. But it would take them a while.

I looked up again. Colonel Jenkins's men were still struggling to climb up the side of the volcano. They were hampered by the fact that their wet boots couldn't gain much traction on the slick plastic surface.

Down below, Sean was being dragged, kicking and screaming, from the Cineplex.

I unfolded my arms, perching on the edge of the volcano.

"No!" Colonel Jenkins cried.

But it was too late. I jumped.

CHAPTER

17

It took them almost half an hour to get me out. The hole in the top of the volcano wasn't that wide. None of the soldiers, let alone Colonel Jenkins, could reach me through it. All my jumping into it accomplished was that it made Colonel Jenkins really mad.

It was worth it.

I sat down there, pretty much comfortably, while they tried to figure out ways to get to me. Finally, someone went over to Sears and bought a power saw, and they cut a big hole in the side of the volcano. They dragged me out, and the people who'd stuck around to watch applauded, like it had all been some big stunt for their benefit.

Special Agents Johnson and Smith were there when they finally dragged me out. They both acted like it was this big personal affront, my taking off the way I had. I did my best to defend myself.

"But I left a note," I insisted as we took off in the carefully nondescript black government vehicle (with tinted windows) that was going to drive us back to Crane, Special Agents Johnson and Smith in the front seat, Sean and I in the back.

"Yes," Special Agent Smith said, "but you took several things with you that led us to believe you weren't coming back."

I demanded to know what those things were. In reply, Special Agent Smith held up the book of photos Colonel Jenkins had left in my room, in hopes of my discovering the whereabouts of a few of its subjects. She'd fished it out of my backpack, which they'd confiscated from me as soon as they'd dug me out of the volcano.

"I was just going to show that to somebody," I said, truthfully. Somewhere in the back of my mind, I'd had this idea—way before Sean had ever called me a dolphin—of taking the book of photos to my brother Michael. I had hoped that, with all his computer skills, he might have been able to find out who the men in it were, using the Internet, or something. I wanted to make sure they were really wanted criminals and not innocent lawyers, like Will Smith in *Enemy of the State*, or something.

Dumb idea, maybe, but then, I'd learned a lesson or two since that morning I'd woken up knowing where Sean was.

"I was going to bring it back," I said.

"Were you?" Special Agent Smith turned to look at me. She seemed particularly disappointed. You could tell she no longer thought I'd be good Bureau material. "If you were planning on coming back, then why'd you take this with you?"

And she pulled my flute, in its wooden case, from my backpack, which she had with her in the front seat.

She had me there, and she knew it.

"When I saw this was missing," she said, illustrating some of the cognitive abilities that had earned her special agent status, "I knew you weren't planning on returning, despite your note and the fact that that bus ticket you bought was for a round-trip."

"Is that how you figured out I was in Paoli?" I asked. I was genuinely interested in learning what my mistakes had been. You know, just in case there was a next time. "The bus ticket?"

"Yes. Clerk at the bus station back by Crane recognized you." Special Agent Johnson, much to my disappointment, drove at exactly the speed limit. It was sickening. All these semis were passing us. With the exception of the band of cars behind us, carrying Colonel Jenkins and his men, ours was the slowest car on the highway. "You aren't exactly an anonymous citizen anymore, Miss Mastriani. Not when you've had your photo on the cover of *Time* magazine."

"Oh," I said. I nodded toward the convoy behind us. "All that firepower, just for little ol' me?"

"You were carrying highly classified data," Special Agent Johnson said, indicating the book of photos. "We just wanted to make sure we got it back."

"But now that you have it back," I said, "you're going to let me go, right?"

"That isn't up to us to decide," Special Agent Johnson said.

"Well, who's it up to?"

"Our superiors."

"The smoking man?"

The agents looked at one another. "Who?" Special Agent Johnson asked.

"Never mind," I said. "Look, can you just tell your superiors that I quit?"

Special Agent Smith looked back at me. She was wearing diamond stud earrings today.

"Jess," she said, "you can't quit."

"Why not?"

"Because you have an extraordinary gift. You have a responsibility to share it with the world." Special Agent Smith shook her head. "I just don't understand where all of this is coming from," she said. "You seemed perfectly happy yesterday, Jess. Why is it that, suddenly, you want to quit?"

I shrugged. Claire Lippman would have been jealous of my acting, I swear. "I guess I'm just homesick."

"Hmmm," Special Agent Johnson said. "I thought the whole reason you changed your mind about coming up here was that you were concerned about your family, that you felt they were being tormented by the media. I thought you felt that leaving them was the only way to give them back some of the privacy they so craved."

I swallowed. "Yeah," I said. "But that was before I got so homesick."

Special Agent Smith shook her head. "Your brother, Douglas. I think they only just released him from the hospital. Seems like, if you went back now, he might just end up there again. All those cameras, flashbulbs going off everywhere—that really shook him up."

That was a low blow. My eyes filled up with tears, and I began seriously to consider flinging myself out the car door—we were certainly going slowly enough that I wouldn't be badly hurt—and making a run for it.

The only problem was that the doors were locked, and the button to unlock them didn't work. The controls were all up in the front seat, by Special Agent Johnson.

And, anyway, I had Sean to think of.

Special Agent Smith was still going on about my responsibility to the world, now that I had this extraordinary gift.

"So I'm supposed to help evil men be brought to justice?" I asked, just to make sure I was clear on things.

"Well, yes," Special Agent Smith said. "And reunite people like Sean here with their loved ones."

Sean and I exchanged glances.

"Hello," Sean said. "Don't you guys read the papers? My dad's a jerk."

"You never really got a chance to know him, now, did you, Sean?" Special Agent Smith said in a soothing voice. "I understand your mother took you from him when you were only six."

"Yeah," Sean said. "Because he'd broken my arm when I didn't put all my toys away one night."

"Jeez," I said, looking at Sean. "Who's your dad, anyway? Darth Vader?"

Sean nodded. "Only not as nice."

"Oh, good job," I said to Special Agents Johnson and Smith. "You two must be real proud of yourselves, reuniting this little boy with a dark lord of the Sith."

"Hey," Sean said, looking appalled. "I'm not little."

"Mr. O'Hanahan," Special Agent Smith said in a tight little voice, "has been declared a fit parent and Sean's rightful guardian by the Illinois state court."

"It used to be legal to have slaves in Illinois, too," Sean said. "But that didn't make it right."

"Courts make mistakes," I said.

"Big ones," Sean said.

I was the only one in the car, I was pretty sure,

who heard his voice shake. I reached out and took his hand. I held it the rest of the way, too, even though it got a little sweaty. Hey, the whole thing was my fault, right? What else was I supposed to do?

They split us up when we got to Crane. Sean had already given everyone the slip once, and I guess they wanted to make extra sure he didn't do it again, so, since his dad wasn't due to pick him up until sometime the next day, they locked him in the infirmary.

I'm not kidding.

I suppose they picked the infirmary, and not, say, the brig, where I think they locked naughty soldiers, because later, they could say he wasn't being held against his will at all . . . after all, they'd given him the run of the infirmary, hadn't they? They'd probably say they locked him in for his own safety.

But even though it wasn't exactly a jail cell, it might as well have been. The windows—there were four of them—were all barred from the outside, I guess to keep people from breaking in and stealing drugs, since the infirmary was on the first floor. And I happened to know, from having been in there the day before for my physical, that all the cabinets with the cool stuff in them, like stethoscopes and hypodermic needles, were locked, and the magazines and stuff were way out of date. Sean wasn't going to have much to keep his mind off his dad's impending arrival.

Me, they locked back into my old room. Seriously. I was right back where I'd started from that morning, with one difference: the door was locked from the outside, and the phone, strangely enough, no longer worked.

I don't know what they thought I was going to do—call the police or something?

"Officer, officer, I'm being held against my will at Crane Military Base!"

"Crane Military Base? What are you talking about? That place closed down years ago!"

No phone privileges for me. And no more trips to the pool, either. My door was very firmly locked.

Marco Polo is locked down for the night. Repeat. Marco Polo is locked down.

Or so they must have thought. But here's the thing:

When you take a kid—who is basically a good kid, but maybe a little quick with her fists—and you make her sit for an hour every day after school with a lot of not-so-good kids, even if she isn't allowed to talk to them during that hour, the fact is, she's going to pick up some things.

And maybe the things she's going to pick up are the kind of things you don't necessarily want a good kid to know. Like, for instance, how to start a really smoky fire in a bus station ladies' room.

Or how to pick a lock. It's pretty easy, actually, depending on the lock. The one to my room

wasn't very tough. I managed to do it with the
ink cartridge from a ballpoint pen.

Look, you just pick these things up, all right?

They caught me right away. Boy, was Colonel
Jenkins mad. But not as mad as Special Agent
Johnson. He'd been viewing me as a thorn in his
side since the day I'd broken his last partner's
nose. You could tell I'd really done it this time.

Which was why they threw the book at me.
They'd really had it. They intended to shut me
up for good this time.

Dr. Shifton did some pleading on my behalf. I
overheard her insisting that I obviously have
issues with authority figures, and that they were
going about this all wrong. I would come around,
she said, when they made it seem like it was my
idea.

Colonel Jenkins didn't like the sound of that.
He went, "Dammit, Helen, she knows the loca-
tion of every single one of those men whose photos we showed her. I can see it in her eyes. What
are we supposed to do, just wait around until
she's in the mood to tell us?"

"Yes," Dr. Shifton said. "That's exactly what
we do."

I liked Dr. Shifton for that. And, anyway, I did
not know where every single one of those men
were.

Just most of them.

I happened to overhear all this because Dr.
Shifton's office is right next to the infirmary, and

that's where they put me after I escaped that second time: in the infirmary, with Sean. . . .

Exactly as I'd wanted them to.

Don't start thinking that I had any sort of plan or anything. I totally didn't. I just figured the kid needed me, is all.

That he didn't happen to agree is really beside the point.

"What are *you* doing here?" he asked, looking up from the bed he was stretched out on. His tone implied he was not pleased to see me.

"Slumming," I said.

"My dad's going to be here first thing in the morning, they said." His face was pinched and white. Well, except for the freckles. "He couldn't make it tonight because of some board meeting. But he gets a police escort tomorrow morning, as soon as he's ready to leave." He shook his head. "That's my dad. Work always comes first. And if you get in the way of that, look out."

I said, gently, "Sean, I said I was going to make it up to you, and I meant it."

Sean looked pointedly at the locked door. "And how are you going to do that?"

"I don't know," I said. "But I will. I swear it."

Sean just shook his head. "Sure," he said. "Sure you will, Jess."

The fact that he didn't believe me just made me more determined.

Hours slid by, and no one came near the infirmary—not even Dr. Shifton. We passed the time trying to figure out ways to escape, listening to talk radio, and doing old *People* magazine crosswords.

Finally, around six o'clock, the door opened, and Special Agent Smith came in, holding a couple of McDonald's bags. I guess my days of surf and turf were over. I didn't care, though. The smell of those fries set my stomach, which I hadn't noticed up until then was quite empty, rumbling noisily.

"Hi," Special Agent Smith said, with a rueful smile. "I brought you guys dinner. You guys okay?"

"Except for the fact that our constitutional rights are being violated," I said, "we're fine."

Special Agent Smith's smile went from rueful to forced. She spread our dinner out on one of the beds: double cheeseburger meals. Not my favorite, but at least she'd super-sized it.

Sean practically inhaled his first burger. I admit to stuffing far more fries into my mouth than was probably good for me. As I stuffed, Special Agent Smith tried her hand at reasoning with me. I guess Dr. Shifton had been coaching her.

"You have a really special gift, Jess," she said. She was practically ignoring Sean. "And it would be a shame to waste it. We need your help so desperately. Don't you want to make this world a safer, better place for kids like yourself?"

"Sure," I said, swallowing. "But I don't want to be a dolphin, either."

Special Agent Smith knit her pretty brow. "A what?"

I told her about the dolphins, while Sean looked on, silently chewing. I'd given him one of my cheeseburgers, but even after three of them, he didn't seem satisfied. He could put away an alarming amount of food for such a small boy.

Special Agent Smith shook her head, still looking perplexed. "I never heard that one before. I know they used German shepherds for similar missions in World War I—"

"German shepherds, dolphins, whatever." I stuck out my chin. "I don't want to be used."

"Jess," Special Agent Smith said. "Your gift—"

"Don't," I said, holding up a single hand. "Seriously. Don't say it. I don't want to hear about it anymore. This 'gift' you keep talking about has caused me nothing but trouble. It sent my brother over the edge, when he'd been doing really well, and it put this little boy's mother in jail—"

"Hey," Sean said indignantly. I'd forgotten about his objections to my use of the word "little" as it related to him.

"Jess." Special Agent Smith balled up the empty bags from my meal. "Be reasonable. It's very sad about Sean's mother, but the fact is, she broke the law. And as for your brother, you can't drop the ball just because of one little setback. Try to keep things in perspective—"

" 'Keep things in perspective'?" I leaned forward and enunciated very carefully so she would be sure to understand me. "Excuse me, Special Agent Smith, but I got struck by lightning. Now, when I go to sleep, I dream about missing people, and it just so happens that when I wake up, I know where those missing people are. Suddenly, the U.S. Government wants to use me as some sort of secret weapon against fugitives from justice, and you think I should *keep things in perspective?*"

Special Agent Smith looked annoyed. "I think you should try to remember," she said, "that what you call a dolphin, most Americans would call a hero."

She turned to throw my empty McDonald's wrappers in the garbage.

"I really didn't come in here," she said, when she turned around again, "to argue with you, Jess. I just thought you might like this back."

She handed me my backpack. The book of photos was gone from it, of course, but my flute was there. I grasped it tightly to my chest.

"Thanks," I said. I was oddly touched by the gesture. Don't ask me why. I mean, it was my flute, after all. I hoped I wasn't beginning to suffer from that thing hostages get, when they start sympathizing with their captors.

"I like you, Jess," Special Agent Smith said. "I really hope that while you're in here tonight, you'll think about what I said. Because you know, I think you'd make a fine federal agent someday."

"Really?" I asked, like I thought this was an enormous compliment.

"I do." She went to the door. "I'll see you two later," she said.

Sean, over on his bed, just grunted. I said, "Sure. Later."

She left. I heard the door lock behind her. The lock on the infirmary door was one that even I, with my extensive knowledge of such things, could not penetrate.

But that didn't matter. Because Special Agent Smith had been right when she'd said I'd make a fine federal agent:

While she'd been throwing out the trash from my meal, I'd reached over and swiped her cell phone from her purse.

I held it up for Sean to see.

"Oh, yeah," I said. "I'm good. *Real* good."

CHAPTER

18

It took us a while to figure out how Special Agent Smith's cell phone worked. Of course there was a password you had to use to get a dial tone. That's what took the longest, figuring out her password. But most passwords, I knew from Michael—who gets his thrills figuring out this kind of thing—are four to six digits or numbers long. Special Agent Smith's first name was Jill. I pressed 5455, and, *voilà*, as my mom would say: we were in.

Sean wanted me to call Channel 11 News.

"Seriously," he said. "They're right outside the gates. I saw them as we drove in. Tell them what's going on."

I said, "Calm down, squirt. I'm not calling Channel 11 News."

He quit bouncing and said, "You know, I'm

getting sick of you calling me squirt and talking about how little I am. I'm almost as tall as you are. And I'll be thirteen in nine months."

"Quiet," I said as I dialed. "We don't have much time before she notices it's gone."

I called my house. My mom picked up. They were eating dinner, Douglas's first since he'd gotten out of the hospital. My mom went, "Honey, how are you? Are they treating you all right?"

I said, "Uh, not exactly. Can I talk to Dad?"

My mom said, "What do you mean, not exactly? Daddy said they had a lovely room for you, with a big TV and your own bathroom. You don't like it?"

"It's okay," I said. "Look, is Dad there?"

"Of course he's here. Where else would he be? And he's as proud of you as I am."

I had been gone only forty-eight hours, but apparently, during the interim, my mother had lost her mind.

"Proud of me?" I said. "What for?"

"The reward money!" my mom cried. "It came today! A check in the amount of ten thousand dollars, made out to you, honey. And that's just the beginning, sweetie."

Man, she had really gone round the bend. "Beginning of what?"

"The kind of income you'll be generating from all of this," my mom said. "Honey, Pepsi called. They want to know if you'd be willing to endorse a new brand of soda they've come up with. It has gingko biloba in it, you know, for brain power."

"You have got," I said, my throat suddenly dry, "to be kidding me."

"No. It's quite good; they left a case here. Jessie, they're offering you a hundred thousand dollars just to stand in front of a camera and say that there are easier ways to expand your brain power than getting struck by lightning—"

In the background I heard my dad say, "Toni." He sounded stern. "She's not doing it."

"Let her make up her own mind, Joe," my mother said. "She might like it. And I think she'll be good at it. Jess is certainly prettier than a lot of those girls I see on the TV—"

My throat was starting to hurt, but there was nothing I could do about it, because all the drugs in the infirmary, even the mouthwash, were locked up.

"Mom," I said. "Can I please talk to Dad?"

"In a minute, honey. I just want to tell you how well Dougie is doing. You're not the only hero in the family, you know. Dougie's doing great, just great. But, of course, he misses his Jess."

"That's great, Mom." I swallowed hard. "That's . . . So, he isn't hearing voices?"

"Not a one. Not since you left and took all those nasty reporters with you. We miss you, sweetie, but we sure don't miss all those news vans. The neighbors were starting to complain. Well, you know the Abramowitzes. They're so fussy about their yard."

I didn't say anything. I don't think I could have spoken if I'd wanted to.

"Do you want to say hi to Dougie, honey? He wants to say hi to you. We're having Dougie's favorite, on account of his being home. Manicotti. I feel bad making it when you aren't here. I know it's your favorite, too. You want me to save you some? Are they feeding you all right up there? I mean, is it just army food?"

"Yeah," I said. "Mom, can I please talk to—"

But my mother had passed the phone to my brother. Douglas's voice, deep but shaky as ever, came on.

"Hey," he said. "How you doing?"

I turned so that I was sitting with my back to Sean, so he wouldn't see me wipe my eyes. "Fine," I said.

"Yeah? You sure? You don't sound fine."

I held the phone away from my face and cleared my throat. "I'm sure," I said, when I thought I could speak without sounding like I'd been crying. "How are you doing?"

"Okay," he said. "They upped my meds again. I've got dry mouth like you wouldn't believe."

"I'm sorry," I said. "Doug, I'm really sorry."

He sounded kind of surprised. "What are you sorry about? It's not your fault."

I said, "Well, yeah. It kind of is. I mean, all those people in our front yard were there on account of me. It stressed you out, having all those people there. And that was my fault."

"That's bull," Douglas said.

But it wasn't. I knew it wasn't. I liked to think that Douglas was a lot saner than my mom gave him credit for being, but the truth was, he was still pretty fragile. Accidentally dumping a tray of plates in a restaurant wasn't going to set off one of his episodes. But waking up to find a whole bunch of strangers with film equipment in his front yard definitely was.

And that's when I knew that, much as I wanted to, I couldn't go home. Not yet. Not if I wanted Douglas to be okay.

"So, are they treating you all right?" Douglas wanted to know.

I stared out between the bars across the windows. Outside, the sun was setting, the last rays of the day slanting across the neatly trimmed lawn. In the distance, I could see a small runway, with a helicopter sitting near it. No helicopters had taken off or landed since I'd been watching. There were no UFOs at Crane. There was no nothing at Crane.

"Sure," I said.

"Really? Because you sound kind of upset."

"No," I said. "I'm okay."

"So. How are you going to spend that reward money?"

"Oh, I don't know. How do you think I should spend it?"

Douglas thought about it. He said, "Well, Dad could use a new set of clubs. Not that he ever gets a chance to play."

"I don't want golf clubs," I heard my dad yelling. "We're putting that money away for Jess's college."

"I want a car!" I heard Michael yell.

I laughed a little. I said, "He just wants a car so he can drive Claire Lippman to the quarries."

Doug said, "You know that's true. And I think Mom would love a new sewing machine."

"So she can make us some more matching outfits." I smiled. "Of course. What about you?"

"Me?" Douglas was beginning to sound even farther away than ever. "I just want you home, and everything back to normal."

I coughed. I had to, in order to cover up the fact that I was crying again.

"Well," I said. "I'll be home soon. And then you'll wish I wasn't, since I'll be barging in on you all the time again."

"I miss you barging in on me," Douglas said.

This was more than I could take. I said, "I . . . I have to go."

Douglas said, "Wait a minute. Dad wants to say—"

But I had hung up. Suddenly, I knew. I couldn't talk to my dad. What was he going to do for me anyway? He couldn't get me out of this.

And even if he could, where was I going to go? I couldn't go home. Not with reporters and

Pepsi representatives following me everywhere I went. Douglas would completely lose whatever fragile grip he had on sanity at the moment.

"Jess?"

I started. I had almost forgotten Sean was in the room with me. I threw him a startled glance.

"What?" I said.

"Are you . . ." He raised his eyebrows. "You are."

"I'm what?"

"Crying," he said. Then his eyebrows met in a rush over the bridge of his freckled nose. He scowled at me. "What are you crying for?"

"Nothing," I said. I reached up and wiped my eyes with the back of my wrist. "I'm not crying."

"You're a damned liar," he said.

"Hey. Don't swear." I began hitting buttons on the phone again.

"Why not? You do it. Who are you calling now?"

"Someone who's going to get us the hell out of here," I said.

CHAPTER

19

It was a little after midnight when I heard it: the same motorcycle engine that I'd been straining my ears to hear on and off for the past couple of weeks. Only this time, it wasn't roaring down Lumley Lane, the way it had in my dreams.

No, it was roaring through the empty parking lots of Crane Military Base.

I leapt up off the bed where I'd been dozing and rushed to the window. I had to cup my fingers over my eyes in order to make out what was going on outside. In a circle of light thrown by one of the security lamps, I saw Rob. He was riding around, his face—hidden by the shield of his motorcycle helmet—turning right and left, trying to figure out which building I was in.

I pounded on the windowpane, and called his name.

Sean, curled up on the bed beside mine, sat bolt upright, as fully awake as he'd been soundly asleep just a second before.

"It's my dad," he said in a choked voice.

"No, it's not your dad," I said. "Stand back while I break this window. He can't hear me."

I knew I only had a few seconds before he thundered past the infirmary. I had to act fast. I grabbed the nearest thing I could find—a metal trash can—and heaved it at the window.

It did the trick. Glass went flying everywhere, including back over me, since a lot of the shards ricocheted off the metal grate. I could feel tiny slivers of glass in my hair and on my shirt.

I didn't care. I yelled, "Rob!"

He threw out a foot and skidded to a halt. A second later, his foot was up again, and he was tearing through the grass toward me. It was only then that I noticed that behind him were about a half dozen other bikers, big guys on Harleys.

"Hey," Rob said when he'd thrown down his kickstand and yanked his helmet off. He got off the bike and came toward me. "You okay?"

I nodded. I can't even tell you how good it felt to see him. It felt even better when he reached through the metal grate, wrapped his fingers around the front of my shirt, dragged me forward, and kissed me through the bars.

When he let go of me, it was so abrupt that I knew he hadn't meant to kiss me at all. It had just sort of happened.

"Sorry," he said—only not looking too sorry, if you know what I mean.

"That's okay," I said. Okay? It was the best kiss I'd ever had—even better than the first one. "Are you sure you don't mind doing this?"

"Piece of cake."

Then he went to work.

Sean, who'd observed the whole thing, said in a very indignant voice, "Who's *that?*"

"Rob Wilkins," I said.

I must have said it a little too happily, however, since Sean asked, suspiciously, "Is he your boyfriend?"

"No," I said. I wish.

Sean was appalled. "And you're just going to let him get away with kissing you like that?"

"He was just glad to see me," I said.

A particularly hairy face had replaced Rob's in the window. I recognized his friend from Chick's, the one with the Tet Offensive tattoo. He snaked a chain through the grate, then secured the other end to the back of one of the bikes.

"Stand back, y'all," he said to us. "This here's gonna make a helluva racket."

The face disappeared. Sean looked up at me.

"These are friends of yours?" he asked, in a disapproving voice.

"Sort of," I said. "Now stand back, will you? I don't want you to get hurt."

"Jesus," Sean muttered. "I am not a baby, all right?"

But when the biker gunned his engine, and the chain rattled, then went taut, Sean clapped his hands over his ears. "We are so busted," he moaned with his eyes closed.

I had a bad feeling Sean was right. The grate was making ominous groaning noises, but not budging so much as an inch. Meanwhile, the motorcycle engine was whining shrilly, its wheels kicking up a ton of dirt, throwing it and bits of grass back through the grate and into the room, already carpeted with glass.

For a minute, I didn't think it was going to work—or that, if it did, the noise would rouse Colonel Jenkins and his men, and they'd be after us in a heartbeat. The grate was simply too deeply embedded into the concrete window frame. I didn't want to say anything, of course— Rob was trying as best he could—but it looked like a hopeless cause. Especially when Sean dug his fingers into my arm and hissed, "Listen. . . ."

Then I heard it. Above the shriek of the motorcycle's engine, the sound of keys rattling outside the infirmary door.

That was it. We were busted.

What was worse, I'd probably gotten our rescuers busted, too. How long would Rob end up in jail because of me? What was the mandatory sentence for trying to break a psychic free from a military compound?

And then, with a sound like a thousand fingernails on a mile-wide chalkboard, the entire grate popped out from the sill and was dragged a few feet until the biker slammed on the brakes.

"Come on," Rob said, reaching for me over the crumbling sill.

I shoved Sean forward. "Him first," I said.

"No, you." Sean, in an effort to be chivalrous, tried to force me through the window first, but Rob got hold of him and hauled him through.

Which gave me a chance to grab my backpack—which Special Agent Smith had so graciously brought me—then vault over the window sill behind them, just as the dead bolt on the infirmary door slid back.

Outside, it was a humid spring night, silent and still . . . except for the thunder of motorcycle engines. I was astonished to see that, in addition to Rob's friends from Chick's, Greg Wylie and Hank Wendell, from the back row of detention, were also there, on majorly cherried-out hogs. I have to admit, I got a little teary-eyed at the sight of them: I had no idea I was so well-liked by my fellow juvenile delinquents.

Sean, however, was not so impressed.

"You have got to be kidding me," he said when he got his first good look at his rescuers.

"Look," I said to him as I pulled on the helmet Rob handed to me. "It's these guys or your dad. Take your pick."

"Boy," Sean said, shaking his head. "You drive a hard bargain."

Hank Wendell shoved a helmet at him. "Here

ya go, kid," he said. He made room on his seat
for Sean's eighty-pound frame, then gave his
engine a rev. "Hop on."

I don't know if Sean would have gotten on if,
at that moment, an eardrum-piercing siren
hadn't begun to wail.

One of the guys from Chick's—Frankie, who
had a tattoo of a baby on his bicep—called out,
"Here they come."

A second later, some military types came running up to the barless window, shouting for us to
stop. Headlights lit up the parking lot.

"Hang on," Rob said as I swung onto the seat
behind him and wrapped my arms around him.

"Halt," a man's voice bellowed. I glanced over
my shoulder. There was a military jeep coming
toward us, with a man standing up in the back,
shouting through a megaphone. Behind him, I
could see lights turning on in the buildings all
across the base, and people running outside, trying to see what was going on.

"This is U.S. Government property," the guy
with the megaphone declared. "You are trespass-
ing. Turn off your engines now."

And then the night air was ripped apart by an
earth-shaking explosion. I saw a ball of flame rise
up in the air over by the airstrip. Everyone
ducked—

Except Frankie and the guy with the Tet
Offensive tattoo, who high-fived one another.

"Oh, yeah," Frankie said. "We still got it."

"What was *that?*" I shouted as Rob accelerated.

"A helicopter," Rob shouted back. "Just a little diversionary tactic, to confuse the enemy."

"You'll blow up a helicopter," I said, "but you won't go out with me?" I couldn't believe it. "What is wrong with you?"

I didn't have a chance to complain for long, however, because Rob sped up, and suddenly we were whipping through the darkened lots that made up Crane, heading for the front gates. The night sky behind us was now filled with an orange glow from the burning helicopter. New sirens, evidently from fire engines sent to put out the flames, sliced through the night, and searchlights arced against the low-lying clouds.

All this, I thought, to bust a small boy and a psychic out of an infirmary.

We hadn't managed to ditch the guy in the jeep. He was right behind us, still shouting through his megaphone for us to stop.

But Rob and his friends didn't stop. In fact, if anything, they sped up.

Okay, I'll admit it: I loved every minute of it. Finally, *finally*, I was going fast enough.

Then, a hundred yards from the front gates, Rob threw his foot out, and we skidded to a halt. His friends followed suit.

For a moment, we sat there, all six bikers, Rob, Sean, and me, engines roaring, staring straight ahead of us. The glow from the fire on the airstrip clearly lit the long road leading to the base's front gates. There were guards there, I remembered from when I'd gone by them on the bus to the mall. Guards with rifles. I had no idea how Rob and the others had gotten past these armed sentries to get onto the base, and I had no idea how we were going to get past them getting off of it. All I could think was, over and over in my head, "Oh, my God, they blew up a helicopter. *They blew up a helicopter.*"

But maybe it was a good thing they did. Because there was no one blocking our path. Everyone was heading toward the airstrip to help put out the fire.

Except for the guy in the jeep behind us.

"Turn off your engines and put your hands up," the guy said.

Instead, Rob lifted up his foot and we lurched forward, heading straight for the gates.

Which were down.

Then someone in a bathrobe came striding across the road, until he stood right in front of the gates. It was someone I recognized. He lifted a megaphone.

"Halt," Colonel Jenkins's voice boomed through the night, louder than the motorcycle engines, louder than the sirens. "You are under arrest. Turn off your engines now."

He was standing directly in front of the gates. His robe had fallen open, and I could see he had on pale blue pajamas.

Rob didn't slow down. If anything, he sped up.

"Turn off your engines," Colonel Jenkins commanded us. "Do you hear me? You are under arrest. Turn off your engines now."

The gatehouse guards appeared with their rifles. They didn't point them at us, but they stood their ground on either side of Colonel Jenkins.

No one turned off their engines. In fact, Greg and Hank let out whoops and started racing even faster toward the gates. I had no idea what they thought was going to happen when they reached the men standing there. It wasn't as if they were simply going to move out of the way and let us by. This was no ordinary game of chicken. Not when the other guy was holding a high-powered rifle.

I guess Colonel Jenkins figured out that nobody was going to turn off his engine, since suddenly he put down the megaphone and nodded to the two guards. I tightened my grip on Rob's waist, and ducked my head, afraid to look. They were only, I was sure, going to shoot into the air, to get our attention. Surely he couldn't mean to—

But then I never did find out whether or not they would have shot at us, because Rob gave the front of the bike a violent jerk. . . .

And then we were sailing off the base. Not through the front gates, but through a wide section of the chain-link fence that had been carefully peeled back to one side of the gates. This was how Rob and his friends had gotten past the sentries. All it had taken was a little determination, a pair of wire cutters, and some experience in breaking-and-entering.

Once we were off the base, the only light we had to see by were the bikes' headlights. That was all right, though. I looked behind me, and saw that the jeep was still behind us, intent on stopping us somehow.

But when I told Rob this, he only laughed. The road that led to Crane was little used, except for traffic to and from the base. All around it were cornfields, and beyond the fields, wooded hills. It was toward these hills Rob plunged, the other bikers following him, veering off the road and into the corn, which this early in spring was only ankle-high.

The jeep bounced along behind us, but it was rough going. The colonel must have gotten the message out, since that single jeep was soon joined by some SUVs. It didn't matter, though. We were darting between them like fireflies. No one could have kept up, except maybe the helicopter, and, well, that wasn't happening, for obvious reasons.

And then we lost them. I don't know if they simply gave up, or were called back to the base, or what. But suddenly, we were on our own.

We had done it.

Still, we stuck to back roads, just to be safe.

I'm pretty sure we weren't followed, though. We stopped several times to check, in sleepy little towns along the way, where there was one gas pump attached to a mom-and-pop general store, and where the noise from the hogs' engines caused bedroom lights to turn on, and dogs chained up in yards to bark.

But there was nothing behind us, nothing except long, empty stretches of road, winding like rivers beneath the heavy sky.

Marco.

Polo.

We were free.

C H A P T E R

20

Rob took us to his house.

Not Greg and Hank and those guys. I have no idea where they went. Well, actually, that's not true. I have a pretty good idea. I think they went to Chick's to pound back a few, and to celebrate their successful penetration of a government facility thought by many to be as impenetrable as Area 51.

Obviously those who thought that had never met anybody from the last row of detention at Ernest Pyle High School.

Sean and I, however, did not join in the festivities. We went to Rob's.

I was surprised when I saw Rob's house. It was a farmhouse, not big—though it was kind of hard to tell in the dark—but built at around the same time as my house on Lumley Lane.

Only, because it was on the wrong side of town, no one had come and put a plaque on it, declaring it a historic landmark.

Still, it was a sweet little house, with a porch out front and a barn out back. Rob lived there with just one other person, his mom. I don't know what happened to his dad, and I didn't want to ask.

We crept into the house very quietly, so as not to wake Mrs. Wilkins, who had recently been laid off from the local plastics factory. Rob showed me his room, and said I could sleep there. Then he gathered up a bunch of blankets and stuff, so that he and Sean could go sleep in the barn.

Sean didn't look particularly happy about this, but then, he was so tired, he could hardly keep his eyes open. He followed Rob around like a little zombie.

I was a little zombie-like myself. I couldn't quite believe what we had done. After I'd gotten undressed, I lay there in Rob's bed, thinking about it. We had destroyed government property. We had defied the orders of a colonel in the United States Army. We had blown up a helicopter.

We were going to be in big trouble in the morning.

Still, I was so sleepy, it was kind of hard to worry about that. Instead, all I could think about was how weird it was to be in a boy's room. At least, a boy who wasn't my brother. I'd been in

Skip's room—you know, over at Ruth's—plenty of times, but it was nothing like Rob's. In the first place, Rob didn't have any posters of Trans Ams up on his walls. Nor did he have any *Playboys* under the bed (I checked). Still, it was pretty alarmingly manly. I mean, he had plaid sheets and stuff.

But his pillow smelled like him, and that was nice, very comforting. I can't tell you what it smelled like, exactly, because that would be too hard to describe, but whatever it was, it was good.

I didn't have a whole lot of opportunity to lie there and enjoy it, though. Because almost as soon as I'd crawled into bed, I fell asleep.

And I didn't wake up again for a long, long time.

When I finally did wake up, it was about noon. It took me a minute to figure out where I was. Then I remembered:

I was in Rob's room, at his house.

And I was wanted by the FBI.

Not just the FBI, either, but the United States Army.

And I wouldn't have been surprised if the Secret Service, the Bureau of Alcohol, Tobacco and Firearms, and the Indiana State Highway Patrol wanted a piece of me, too.

And, interestingly, from the moment I woke up, I knew exactly what I was going to do about it.

It's not every day a girl wakes up knowing

she's wanted by the federal law enforcement agency of the most powerful country in the world. I thought about lying around, relishing it, but I was kind of worried about the impression that would make on Mrs. Wilkins, who could, if I played my cards right, be my mother-in-law someday. I didn't want her thinking I was this big slacker or something, so instead I got up, got dressed, and went downstairs.

Sean and Rob were already there, sitting at the kitchen table. In front of them was one heck of a lot of food. There was toast, and eggs, and bacon, and cereal, and a bowl of some white stuff I could not identify. The plate in front of Rob was empty—he was apparently through eating. But Sean was still putting it away. I don't think he'll ever be through eating. At least, not until after he's done going through puberty.

"Hi, Jess," he said when I walked into the kitchen. He sounded—and looked—a good deal perkier than he had during the last twenty-four hours I'd spent with him.

"Hi," I said.

A plump woman standing by the stove turned and smiled at me. She had a lot of red hair piled up on top of her head with a barrette, and didn't look a thing like her son Rob.

Until a shaft of sunlight, coming through the window above the sink, lit her face, and I saw that she had his eyes, so light blue they were the color of fog.

"You must be Jess," she said. "Pull up a chair and sit yourself down. How do you like your eggs?"

"Um," I said, awkwardly. "Scrambled is fine, thank you, ma'am."

"The eggs are fresh," Sean informed me as I sat down. "From the henhouse out back. I helped gather them."

"Your friend Sean's turning into a real farm-hand," Mrs. Wilkins said. "We'll have him milk-ing, next."

Sean giggled. I blinked at him. He'd actually *giggled.*

That was when I realized, with a shock, that I had never seen him happy before.

"There you go," Mrs. Wilkins said, setting a plate down in front of me. "Now you eat up. You look as if you could use a good hearty country breakfast."

I had never had fresh eggs before, and I was kind of worried they'd have some half-formed chicken fetus in them, but they didn't. They were really delicious, and when Mrs. Wilkins offered seconds, I gladly took them. I was pretty hungry, I discovered. I even ate some of the white stuff Mrs. Wilkins glopped onto my plate. It tasted like the Cream of Wheat my father always made us eat before school on really cold days when we were little.

But it wasn't Cream of Wheat. It was, Rob informed me with a little smile, grits.

If Ruth could only see me now, I thought.

After I'd helped Mrs. Wilkins wash the breakfast dishes, however, the fun was over. It was time to get down to business.

"I need to use a phone," I announced, and Mrs. Wilkins pointed to hers, hanging on the wall by the refrigerator.

"You can use that one," she said.

"No," I said. "For this particular call, I think I better use a pay phone."

Rob eyed me suspiciously. "What's up?" he wanted to know.

"Nothing," I said, innocently. "I just need to make a call. Is there a pay phone around here?"

Mrs. Wilkins looked thoughtful. "There's the one down the road, over by the IGA," she said.

"Perfect." To Rob, I said, "Can you drive me over there?"

He said he could, and we got up to go. . . .

And so did Sean.

"Nuh-uh," I said. "No way. You stay here."

Sean's jaw dropped. "What do you mean?"

"I mean there are probably cops crawling all over the place, looking for a sixteen-year-old girl in the company of a twelve-year-old boy. They'll be on to us in a second. You stay here until I get back."

"But that's not fair," Sean declared, his voice breaking.

I felt of bubble of impatience well up inside me. But instead of snapping at him, I grabbed

Sean by the arm and steered him out onto the back porch.

"Look," I said softly, so Rob and his mother wouldn't hear. "You said you wanted things back the way they were, didn't you? You and your mom, together, without your dad breathing down your necks?"

"Yes," Sean admitted, sullenly.

"Well, then let me do what I have to do. Which is something I have to do alone."

Sean was right about one thing: He was small for his age, but he really wasn't little. He wasn't even all that shorter than me. Which was how he was able to look me straight in the eye and say, accusingly, "That guy really is your boyfriend, isn't he?"

Where had *that* come from?

"No, Sean," I said. "I told you. We're just friends."

Sean brightened considerably. He said, "Okay," and went back inside.

Men. I swear I just don't get it.

Ten minutes later, I was standing in front of a little general store, the handset to an ancient pay phone pressed to my ear. I dialed carefully.

1-800-WHERE-R-YOU.

I asked for Rosemary, and when she came on, I said, "Hey, it's me. Jess."

"Jess?" Rosemary's voice dropped to a whisper. "Oh, my goodness. Is that really you?"

"Sure," I said. "Why?"

"Honey, I've been hearing all sorts of things on the news about you."

"Really?" I looked over at Rob. He was refilling the Indian's tank from the single pump in front of the store. We hadn't watched the news yet, and Mrs. Wilkins didn't get any newspapers, so I was eager to hear what they were saying about me. "What kind of stuff?"

"Well, about how last night, a group of Hell's Angels tore up Crane Military Base and kidnapped you and little Sean O'Hanahan off of it, of course."

"WHAT?" I yelled, so loud that Rob looked over at me. "That's not how it happened at all. Those guys were helping us to escape. Sean and I were being held against our will."

Rosemary said, "Well, that's not how that fellow—what's his name? Johnson, I think. That's not how Special Agent Johnson is telling it. There's a reward out for your safe return, you know."

This sounded interesting. "How much?"

"Twenty thousand dollars."

"Each?"

"No, that's just for you. Sean's father posted a hundred thousand dollar reward for his return."

I nearly hung up, I was so disgusted. "Twenty thousand dollars? Twenty piddling thousand dollars? That's all I'm worth to them? That loser. That's it. This is war."

Rosemary said, "I'd look out if I were you,

honey. There's APBs out all over the state of Indiana. Folks are looking for you."

"Oh, yeah, I bet. Listen, Rosemary," I said, "I want you to do me a favor."

Rosemary said, "Anything, hon."

"Give Agent Johnson a message for me. . . ."

Then I carefully stated the message I wanted Rosemary to relay.

"Okay," she said, when I was through. "You got it, honey. And, Jess?"

I had been about to hang up. "Yes?"

"You hang in there, honey. We're all behind you."

I hung up and told Rob about Special Agent Johnson's bogus kidnapping story—not to mention the crummy reward out for my capture. Rob was as mad as I was. Now that we knew there was an APB out on me, and that Hell's Angels were being blamed for what had happened at Crane, we agreed it wasn't a good idea for me to be seen tooling around on the back of Rob's bike. So we hurried back to his mom's place—but not until after I'd made one last call, this one from a pay phone outside a 7-Eleven on the turnpike.

My dad was where he usually is at lunchtime: Joe's. They get quite a noon crowd from the courthouse.

"Dad," I said. "It's me."

He nearly choked on his rigatoni, or whatever the special for the day was. My dad always taste-tests.

"Jess?" he cried. "Are you all right? Where are you?"

"Of course I'm all right," I said. "Now, anyway. Look, Dad, I need you to do me a favor."

"What are you talking about?" my dad demanded. *Where are you?* Your mother and I have been worried sick. The folks up at Crane are saying—"

"Yeah, I know. That a bunch of Hell's Angels kidnapped Sean and me. But that's bogus, Dad. Those guys were rescuing us. Do you know what they were trying to do, Special Agents Johnson and Smith, that Colonel Jenkins guy? They were trying to make me into a dolphin."

My dad sounded like he was choking some more. "A *what?*"

Rob poked me hard in the back. I turned around to see what he wanted, and was horrified when an Indiana State Police patrol car eased into the parking lot of the convenience store.

"Look, Dad," I said, quickly ducking my head. "I gotta go. I just need you to do this one thing for me."

And I told him what the one thing was.

My dad wasn't too thrilled about it, to say the least.

He went, "Have you lost your mind? You listen here, Jessica—"

Nobody in my family ever calls me Jessica, except when they are really peeved at me.

"Just do it, please, Dad?" I begged. "It's really

important. I'll explain everything later. Right now, I gotta go."

"Jessica, don't you—"

I hung up.

Rob had drifted away from me, distancing himself and his bike from the teenage girl at the pay phone, in case the cops made a connection. But it didn't look as if they had. One of them even nodded to me as he went into the store.

"Nice day," he said.

As soon as they were inside, Rob and I made a mad dash for his bike. We were already at the turnpike by the time they realized what they'd missed and came hurtling out of the store. I looked back over my shoulder and saw their mouths moving as we tore away. A few seconds later, they were in their car, sirens blaring.

I hung onto Rob more tightly. "We've got company," I said.

"Not for long," Rob said.

And suddenly we were off-road, brambles and sticks tearing at our clothing as we plunged down a ravine. Seconds later, we were splashing through a creekbed, the Indian's front wheel kicking up thick streams of water on either side of it. Above us, I could see the patrol car following along as best it could. . . .

But then the creek made a bend away from the road, and soon the cop car disappeared from view. Soon I couldn't even hear its siren anymore.

When Rob finally pulled out of the creekbed and back up the ravine, I was wet from the waist down, and the Indian's engine was sounding kind of funny.

But we were safe.

"You all right?" Rob asked me, as I was wringing out the bottom of my T-shirt.

"Peachy," I said. "Listen, I'm sorry."

He was squatting beside the bike's front wheel, pulling out sticks and weeds that had wound into the spokes during our flight down the ravine. "Sorry about what?"

"Getting you involved in all this. I mean, I know you're on probation and all. The last thing you need is to be harboring a couple of fugitives. What if you get caught? They'll probably lock you up and throw away the key. I mean, depending on whatever it is you did to get on probation in the first place."

Rob had moved to the back tire. He squinted up at me, the afternoon sun bringing out the strong planes in his face. "Are you through?"

"Through what?"

"Through trying to trick me into telling you what I'm on probation for."

I put my hands on my hips. "I am not trying to trick you into doing anything. I am merely trying to let you know that I am aware of the great personal sacrifice you are making in helping Sean and me, and I appreciate it."

"You do, huh?"

He straightened. One of the sticks he'd wrenched from the wheel had flicked drops of water up onto his face, so he pulled the bottom of his T-shirt out from the waistband of his jeans and scrubbed at them. When he did this, I happened to get a look at his bare stomach. The sight of it, all tightly muscled, with a thin band of dark hair down the center, did something to me.

I don't know what came over me, but suddenly, I was on my tiptoes, planting this big wet one on him. I have seriously never done anything like that before, but I just couldn't help it.

Rob seemed a little surprised at first, but he got over it pretty quickly. He kissed me back for a while, and it was just like in *Snow White* when all the woodland animals come out and start singing, and Prince Charming puts her up on the horse. For about a minute it was like that. I mean, my heart was singing just like one of those damned squirrels.

Then Rob reached up and started untangling my arms from around his neck.

"Jesus, Mastriani," he said. "What are you trying to do?"

That broke the spell pretty quick, let me tell you. I mean, Prince Charming would never have said something like that. I would have been mad if I hadn't heard the way his voice shook.

"Nothing," I said, very innocently.

"Well, you better cut it out," he said. "We've got a lot do. There's no time for any distractions."

I mentioned that I happened to like that particular distraction.

Rob went, "I'm in enough trouble right now without you adding to it, thanks." He picked up one of the helmets and shoved it down over my head. "And don't even think about trying something like that in front of the kid."

"What kid? What are you talking about?"

"The kid. O'Hanahan. What are you, blind, Mastriani? He's got it bad for you."

I tilted the helmet back and squinted at him. "*Sean? For me?*"

But all of a sudden, all the questions he'd been asking about Rob made sense.

I let the helmet drop back over my face. "Oh, God," I said.

"You got that right. He thinks you are one dope girl, Mastriani."

"He said that? He sure doesn't act like he thinks that. He really said I was dope?"

"Well." Rob swung onto his seat and gave the accelerator a kick. "I might be allowing my own feelings to cloud the matter a little."

Suddenly, all the birds and squirrels were singing again.

"You think I'm dope?" I asked dreamily.

He reached out and flicked my helmet. It made a hollow echoing sound inside my head, and brought me right out of my reverie.

"Get on the bike, Mastriani," he said.

When we got back to Rob's, Sean and Mrs.

Wilkins were shelling peas and watching Ricki Lake.

"Jess," he said when I walked in. "Where have you been? You totally missed this guy. He weighed four hundred pounds and got stuck in a bathtub for over forty-eight hours! If you'd been here sooner, you could have seen it."

It was love. I could totally tell.

This was going to be harder than I thought.

CHAPTER

21

The marching band was playing "Louie, Louie."

And not very well, I might add.

Still, Sean and I stayed where we were, sitting on the same metal bleachers that a week or so before I'd been electrocuted under. Before us stretched the football field, a sea of luscious green, upon which marched a herd of musicians playing for all they were worth, even though it was only an after-school rehearsal, and not the real thing. Football season was long over, but graduation was coming up, and the band would play at commencement.

Just not "Louie, Louie," hopefully.

"I don't get it," Sean said. "What are we doing here?"

"Wait," I said. "You'll see."

We weren't the only spectators in the stands. There was one other guy, way, way up at the top behind us.

But that was it. I wasn't sure if Rosemary had failed to get my message to Special Agent Johnson, or if he'd chosen merely to ignore it. If he was ignoring it, he was making a grave mistake. The guy up in the stands would make sure of that.

"Why won't you tell me what we're doing here?" Sean demanded. "I think I have a right to know."

"Drink your Big Gulp," I said. It was hot out. The late afternoon sun was beating down on us. I didn't have any sunglasses or a hat, and I was dying. I was worried Sean might be getting dehydrated.

"I don't want my stupid Big Gulp," Sean said. "I want to know what we're doing here."

"Watch the band," I said.

"The band sucks." Sean glared at me. Most of the brown had washed out of his hair when he'd showered at Rob's. It was a good thing he'd let Mrs. Wilkins give him a trim, or the bits of red sticking out of the back of his baseball cap would have been a dead giveaway.

"What are we doing here?" he wanted to know. "And why is Jed waiting down there?"

Jed turned out to be the name of Rob's friend from Chick's, the one who'd been in Vietnam. He was sitting in a pickup not far from us, parked over behind the bleachers . . . almost exactly, in fact, in the place where I'd been struck by lightning. It was shady where he was. He probably didn't feel sweat prickling all along his hairline, the way I did.

"Just cool it, will you?" I said to Sean.

"No, I will not cool it, Jess. I think I deserve an explanation. Are you going to give me one or not?"

Something caught the sunlight and winked at me. I shaded my eyes and looked toward the parking lot. A black, nondescript sedan had pulled up.

"Louie, Louie" ended. The band started a spirited rendition of Robert Palmer's "Simply Irresistible."

"How come you aren't in Band?" Sean wanted to know. "I mean, you play the flute and all. How come you're not in Band?"

The car pulled up to a halt. The two front doors opened, and a man and a woman got out. Then a back door opened, and another woman got out.

"Because I'm in Orchestra," I said.

"What's the difference?"

"In Orchestra, you play sitting down."

"That's it?"

The man and woman from the front seats moved until they stood on either side of the woman who'd gotten out of the backseat. Then they started walking across the football field, toward Sean and me.

"The Orchestra doesn't play at school events," I said. "Like games and stuff."

Sean digested this. "Where do you play, then?"

"Nowhere. We just have concerts every once in a while."

"What's the fun in that?" Sean wanted to know.

"I don't know," I said. "I couldn't be in Band, anyway. I'm always in detention when they practice."

"Why are you always in detention?"

"Because I do a lot of bad stuff."

The trio moving across the football field had gotten close enough for me to see that they were who I was expecting. Rosemary had gotten my message across, all right.

"What kind of bad stuff?" Sean wanted to know.

"I hit people." I reached into the back pocket of my jeans.

"So?" Sean looked indignant. "They probably deserve it."

"I like to think so," I said. "Look, Sean, I want you to take this. It's for you and your mom. Jed's going to drive you to the airport. I want you guys to get on a plane—any plane—and take off. Don't make any calls. Don't stop for anything. You can buy whatever you need when you get to where you're going. Understand?"

Sean looked down at the envelope I was holding out to him. Then he looked up at me.

"What are you talking about?" he asked.

"Your mom," I said. "You two are going to have to start over, somewhere else. Somewhere far away, I hope, where your dad won't be able to find you. This will help you get started." I tucked the envelope into the front pocket of his jean jacket.

Sean shook his head. His face was tight with emotion. Conflicting emotions, from the looks of it. "Jess. My mom's in jail. Remember?"

"Not anymore," I said. And then I pointed.

The three people approaching us were close enough now that I could make out their features. Special Agent Johnson, Special Agent Smith, and between them, a slim woman in blue jeans. Sean's mother.

He looked. I heard him inhale sharply.

Then he turned to stare at me. The conflicting emotions on his face weren't so hard to make out now. There was joy, mingled with concern.

"What did you do?" he whispered. "Jess. What did you do?"

"I cut a little deal," I said. "Don't worry about it. Just go get her, and then go and get into the pickup with Jed. He'll take you to the airport."

Even as I sat there, looking down at him, his blue eyes filled with tears.

He said, "You did it. You said you'd do it. And you did it."

"Of course," I said, as if I was shocked he could ever have thought otherwise.

And then his mother saw him and broke away from her escorts. She called Sean's name as she ran toward him.

Sean leapt up and began hurtling down the bleachers. I stayed where I was. Sean had left his Big Gulp behind. I reached over and took a sip. My throat really hurt, for some reason.

They met at the bottom of the bleachers. Sean flung himself into Mrs. O'Hanahan's arms. She swung him around. Special Agents Johnson and Smith stopped where they were, and looked up at me. I waved. They didn't wave back.

Then Sean said something to his mother, and she nodded. The next thing I knew, he was running back toward me.

This had not been part of the plan. I stood up, alarmed.

"Jess," Sean cried, panting, as he hurried to my side.

"What are you doing here?" I asked, more sharply than I should have. "Go back to her. I told you to take her to the pickup. Hurry up, you don't have much time—"

"I just . . ." He was breathing so hard, he had to fight to get the words out. "I wanted . . . to say . . . thank you."

And then he threw his arms around my neck.

I didn't know what to do at first. I was pretty surprised. I looked down at the football field. The agents were still standing there, looking up at me. The band launched into a new song. The Beatles' "Hard Day's Night."

I hugged Sean back. My throat hurt even worse, and my eyes stung.

Allergies, I thought.

"When am I going to see you again?" Sean wanted to know.

"You're not," I said. "Not unless things change. You know, with your dad. Don't you dare call me otherwise. They'll probably be tapping my phone forever."

"What about—" He broke away from me and looked at me. His eyes were streaming as badly as mine. "What about when I'm thirty? You'll be thirty-three. It wouldn't be so weird, would it, a thirty-year-old going out with a thirty-three-year-old?"

"No," I said, giving the brim of his baseball cap a tap. "Except when you're thirty, I'll be thirty-four. You're only twelve, remember?"

"Just for nine more months."

I kissed him on his wet cheek. "Get out of here," I said.

He managed a watery smile. Then he turned around and ran away again. This time when he got to his mother's side, he took her hand and started dragging her around the side of the bleachers, to where Jed waited.

Only after I heard the engine start up and the truck pull away did I make my own way down the bleachers—making sure I'd wiped my eyes first.

Special Agent Johnson looked hot in his suit and tie. Special Agent Smith seemed a bit cooler in her skirt and silk blouse, but not by much. Standing there together like that, in their sunglasses and nice clothes, they made kind of a cute couple.

"Hey," I said as I sauntered up to them. "Do you two have an *X-Files* thing going?"

Special Agent Smith looked down at me. She had on her pearl earrings today. "I beg your pardon?" she said.

"You know. One of those Scully/Mulder things. Do you burn for one another with a passion that must be denied?"

Special Agent Johnson looked at Special Agent Smith. "I'm married, Jessica," he said.

"Yes," Special Agent Smith said. "And I'm seeing someone."

"Oh." I felt strangely let-down. "Too bad."

"Well." Special Agent Johnson peered at me expectantly. "Do you have the list?"

I nodded. "Yeah, I've got it. Do I have your word that nobody is going to try to stop Sean and his mother at the airport?"

Special Agent Smith looked offended. "Of course."

"Or when they get to where they're going?"

Special Agent Johnson said, impatiently, "Jessica, nobody cares about the child and his mother. It's the list we want."

I gave him a very mean look. "*I* care about

them," I said. "And I'm sure Mr. O'Hanahan isn't going to be too happy when he finds out."

"Mr. O'Hanahan," Special Agent Smith said, "is our problem, not yours. The list, please, Jessica."

"And nobody's going to press any charges?" I asked, just to make sure. "About the whole Crane thing? Against me or anybody else?"

"No," Agent Johnson said.

"Even about the helicopter?"

"Even," Agent Johnson said, and I could tell his teeth were gritted, "about the helicopter."

"The list, Jessica," Special Agent Smith said, again. And this time she held out her hand.

I sighed, and dug into my back pocket. The band launched into a particularly corny version of "We're the Kids in America."

"Here you go," I said, and surrendered a crumpled sheet of paper into the agent's hand.

Special Agent Smith unfolded the paper and scanned it. She looked down at me disapprovingly.

"There are only four addresses on here," she said, handing the paper to her partner.

I stuck out my chin. "What do you think?" I demanded. "I'm not a machine. I'm just a kid. There'll be more where those came from, don't worry."

Special Agent Johnson folded the sheet of paper back up and stuck it in his pocket.

"All right," he said. "What now?"

"You two go back to your car and drive away," I said.

"And you?" Special Agent Smith asked.

"I'll be in touch," I said.

Special Agent Smith chewed her lower lip. Then she said, as if she couldn't help it, "You know, it didn't have to be this way, Jess."

I looked at her. I couldn't read her eyes behind her dark glasses.

"No, it didn't," I said. "Did it?"

She and Special Agent Smith exchanged glances. Then they turned around and started the long walk back to their car.

"You know," I called after them. "No offense to Mrs. Johnson and all, but you two really do make a cute couple."

They just kept walking.

"That was pushing it, don't you think?" Rob asked, as he crawled out from underneath the bleachers, where he'd been stationed the whole time.

"I'm just messing with them," I said.

Rob brushed dust off his jeans. "Yeah," he said. "I noticed. You do that a lot. So are you going to tell me what was in that envelope?"

"The one I gave to Sean?"

"The one you gave to Sean after you made me pick it up from your dad. Who, by the way, hates me."

I noticed there was some dust on his black T-shirt, too. This gave me a good excuse to touch his chest as I brushed it off.

"My dad can't possibly hate you," I said. "He doesn't even know you."

"He sure looked like he hated me."

"That's just because of what was in the envelope."

"Which was?"

"The ten grand I got as a reward for finding Olivia Marie D'Amato."

Rob whistled, low and long. "You gave that kid ten grand? In *cash*?"

"Well, him and his mother. I mean, they have to have something to live on while she finds a new job and everything."

Rob shook his head. "You are one piece of work, Mastriani," he said. "Okay. So that's what was in the envelope. What was on that sheet of paper you handed to the Feds?"

"Oh," I said. "Just the addresses of some of America's most wanted. I said I'd give them up in return for the charges against Mrs. O'Hanahan being dropped."

"Really?" Rob seemed surprised. "I thought you didn't want to get involved in all of that."

"I don't. That's why I only gave them the addresses of the guys from that book of theirs who happen to be deceased."

A slow smile crept over Rob's face. "Wait a minute. You—"

"I didn't lie or anything. They really will find those guys where I said they'd be. Well, what's left of them, anyway." I wrinkled my nose. "I have a feeling it's not going to be pretty."

Rob shook his head again. Then he reached

out and put an arm around my shoulders. "Jess," he said, "you make me proud to have sat by you in detention. Did you know that?"

I smiled sunnily at him. "Thanks," I said. Then I looked up at the lone figure still sitting in the bleachers, high above our heads.

"Come on," I said, taking Rob's hand. "There's still one more thing I have to do."

Rob looked up at the guy in the stands. "Who's that?" he asked.

"Who, him? Oh, that's the guy who's going to set me free."

CHAPTER

22

I probably don't have to tell you the rest. I mean, I'm sure you've already read about it, or seen it on the news, or something.

But just in case, here goes:

The story came out the next day. It was on the front page of the *Indianapolis Star*. Rob and I had to pick up a copy from the Denny's down the highway from his mother's house. Then we ordered a Grand Slam breakfast and ate while we read.

Lightning Girl Claims to Have Run Out of Juice, the headline ran. Then there was a story all about me, and how I had tragically lost my power to find people.

Just like that, I'd told the reporter that day in the bleachers. He'd been so excited about his scoop, he'd eaten up every word, hardly even asking a single question.

I just woke up, I said, and it was gone. I'm a normal girl again.

End of story.

Well, it wasn't quite the end, of course. Because the reporter asked me a lot of searching questions about what had happened at Crane. I assured him that the whole thing had been a misunderstanding, that the alleged Hell's Angels were actually my friends, and that after my special power had disappeared, I had gotten homesick, so I'd called them, and they'd come to pick me up. I had no idea why that helicopter had blown up. But it was a good thing nobody had been in it at the time, wasn't it?

And the O'Hanahan boy? the reporter had asked. What had happened to him?

I said I had no idea. I'd heard, just as the reporter had, about Sean's mother being mistakenly released from jail. Yes, I could imagine Mr. O'Hanahan had been plenty mad about that.

But wherever Sean and his mother were, I told the reporter, I wished them well.

The reporter didn't look as if he believed this, but he was so excited to be breaking the story, he didn't care. The only conditions I gave him were that he didn't mention Rob's or his mother's names.

The reporter didn't let me down. He got the story exactly the way I wanted it, and even put in some quotes from the people at Crane, whom he'd called after interviewing me. Dr. Shifton he reported as being relieved I was all right. It wasn't at all unusual, she said, that my mysterious power had vanished just as suddenly as it had appeared. It often worked that way with lightning-strike victims.

Colonel Jenkins wasn't quoted anywhere in the article, but Special Agent Johnson was, and he said some nice things about me, and about how I had used my special gift to help others, which was admirable, and how he hoped that if my powers ever came back I'd call him.

Ha. As if.

Finally, the reporter interviewed my parents, who sounded bewildered, but happy to know I was all right. "We just can't wait," my mother said, "to have our baby back home, and everything back to normal again."

You'd be surprised how fast everything did go back to normal. The *Star* broke the story, and by later that night, every newscast mentioned something about the "lightning girl" and how she'd lost her special missing-child finding skill.

By the next day, the story had moved to the "Lifestyle" section of most papers, in the form of reflections on the part of columnists on the hidden powers of the brain and how all of us have the potential to be a "lightning girl," if we just pay attention to what our subconscious is trying to tell us.

Yeah, right.

By the day after that, the reporters in front of

my house had packed up and left. It was safe. I could go home.

And so I did.

Well, that's pretty much my "statement." My hand is really tired. I hope this "statement" is long enough. But if it isn't, I don't really care. I'm hungry, and I want dinner. Mom promised to make manicotti, which is Douglas's favorite, and mine, too. Also, I have to practice. Monday after school I have to defend my chair in Orchestra from Karen Sue Hanky.

My one regret about all this is that there are only a few weeks of school left, and since detention is the only place I'll ever see Rob, this is a problem. In spite of everything, I still haven't been able to convince him that going out with me would not be a crime.

I haven't given up, though. I can be very persuasive when I put my mind to it.

Now that I've read back over this statement, I'm not so sure anymore that all of this is Ruth's fault. The fact that I got struck by lightning, maybe. On the other hand, Ruth never would have wanted to walk home that day if it hadn't been for Jeff telling her she was as fat as Elvis. So maybe it's all Jeff's fault.

Yeah, I think it is. Jeff Day's fault, I mean.

Signed:

Jessica Antonia Mastriani

To: Cyrus Krantz
    Special Operations Division
Fr: Special Agent Allan Johnson
Re: Special Subject Jessica Mastriani

What you have just read is the signed personal statement of Special Subject Jessica Mastriani. According to Miss Mastriani, her psychic powers ceased functioning on or about April 27—coincidentally, the morning after her escape from Crane. It is the opinion of this operative, however, that Miss Mastriani maintains full possession of her extraordinary powers, as illustrated by the following.

In the six weeks following Miss Mastriani's return to private life, 1-800-WHERE-R-YOU has received approximately one anonymous tip per week that has led to the successful recovery of a missing child. All of these calls have been received by Mrs. Rosemary Atkinson, a receptionist with whom Miss Mastriani seems to have developed a relationship during her initial con-

tact with the NOMC. Mrs. Atkinson denies that
the anonymous caller is Miss Mastriani. However, all of the calls have been made from pay
phones within Indiana state lines.

Additionally, the day after the completion of
the attached statement, Miss Mastriani received
at her home a single postcard, bearing on it a
photo of several dolphins. The postmark indi-
cated that the card was mailed from Los Angeles.
When questioned by her mother as to the iden-
tity of the anonymous sender, Miss Mastriani
replied, within hearing of our positioned operative, "It's from Sean. He just wants to let me
know where he is. Which is stupid, because I'll
always know where he is."

It is the feeling of this operative that Miss
Mastriani continues to maintain full possession of
her psychic ability. I am hereby requesting autho-
rization to continue monitoring Miss Mastriani,
including tapping of her home telephone as well
as the telephones of her father's restaurants.
Should Miss Mastriani be proved to have been less
than truthful in her submitted statement, this operative suggests utilizing her relationship with the
mentally disturbed sibling as a form of persuasion
in enlisting her aid on our behalf.

I look forward to your positive response to
this request.